D1502345

THE LAW'S DELAY

'It's a case of murder,' said Horton.

Antony Maitland sighed. 'Your client, I suppose, being the murderer,' he said.

'Well, I think so. It's a woman ... Ellen Gray.'

The trial of Ellen Gray for murder comes early in the story. She is defended by Antony Maitland, Q.C. and the jury's verdict surprises both Ellen and Antony.

This murder has been committed in 1965. But it is evident to Antony that its motivation derives from a bizarre double-murder in 1946, when a woman and her lover had been shot dead by a jealous husband returning from the war; at least, that was the historical record.

Antony began to doubt the whole history. He began to think it odd that two murderers should have been found among the same small group, even if the crimes were nearly twenty years apart. So it is on this small group, the tight-knit clique who were friends in the forties, that his attention increasingly falls.

Then Antony Maitland moves from the role of barrister to that of detective, as he has done before. Supported by his wife, Jenny, aided by his friend Roger Farrell (and as always derided by his formidable uncle, Sir Nicholas Harding, Q.C.), he seeks solutions to the murders quite different from past convictions and police thinking. And at last, in a surprising and convincing dénouement, he finds an answer.

Sara Woods's histories of the cases of Antony Maitland have held a wide readership for many years. She is at her strongest and most ingenious here, in the setting up and unravelling of two sets of murders twenty years apart.

By the same author

MY LIFE IS DONE

36934

THE LAW'S DELAY

SARA WOODS

For who would bear the whips and scorns of time,
The oppressor's wrong, the proud man's contumely,
The pangs of dispriz'd love, the law's delay...

Hamlet, Act III, scene i

VON CANON LIBRARY
SOUTHERN SEMINARY
BUENA VISTA, VIRGINIA 24416

ST. MARTIN'S
NEW YORK

Copyright © 1977 by Sara Woods

All rights reserved. For information, write:
St. Martin's Press, Inc., 175 Fifth Ave.,
New York, N.Y. 10010

Library of Congress Catalog Card Number: 76-28070

First published in the United States of America in 1977

Printed in Great Britain

Any work of fiction whose characters were of uniform
excellence would rightly be condemned – by that fact
if by no other – as being incredibly dull. Therefore no
excuse can be considered necessary for the villainy or
folly of the people appearing in this book. It seems
extremely unlikely that any one of them should resemble
a real person, alive or dead. Any such resemblance is
completely unintentional and without malice.

S.W.

PR 6073 .063 L38 1977

There was once a case on which Antony Maitland worked in comparative amity with Detective Inspector Conway, but at the time when the events related in this story took place that happy state of affairs was still in the future, and could not be foreseen.

S.W.

PART ONE

HILARY TERM

1965

WEDNESDAY, 13th January

It had been a long day in court, bad luck to be caught by so complex a case so early in the term. When they came out into the Strand it was still a toss up whether he would go back to chambers or straight home, but after a moment's indecision Antony Maitland loaded his companion with the books he had been carrying under his arm and began to look about for a taxi. Willett, who already had a good armful of files, grinned cheerfully, said, 'See you tomorrow,' and darted across the road among the traffic, leaving Maitland reflecting gratefully that the clerk seemed impervious to late hours, or for that matter to any other of the slings and arrows that outrageous fortune might have in store for him.

At that hour the traffic was heavy, and it was a relief when a cruising taxi caught his signal and swerved dangerously across the front of a Daimler limousine to pick him up. He said, 'Five, Kempenfeldt Square,' and leaned well back, stretching out his legs with a sense of luxury. He had done as much work as he could on the fraud case, nothing now to worry about until he began to call his witnesses on the morrow. It would be good to get home.

Antony and Jenny Maitland lived, as they had done since the end of the war when accommodation was scarce, in the top half of Sir Nicholas Harding's house in Kempenfeldt Square. Sir Nicholas was Antony's uncle, as well as the head of the chambers to which, as a barrister, he belonged, and the arrangement – embarked on as a temporary measure – was so convenient that they had

9

none of them ever seriously thought of changing it. Now, as he paid off the taxi, Antony eyed uneasily the cars that were parked along the kerb. One of them, a rather elderly Austin in a beautiful state of preservation, looked familiar. It was with a sense of foreboding that he mounted the steps, found his latchkey, and let himself in.

Sure enough, Gibbs was hovering at the back of the hall, waiting for him. Gibbs was Sir Nicholas's butler, a disagreeable old man who refused to be retired but enjoyed making a martyrdom of his extended service. He said now, gloomily, 'Mr Horton is waiting for you, Mr Maitland. I took him upstairs.' His tone seemed to rebuke Antony's tardiness.

'Thank you.' That was that, then. And he liked Geoffrey Horton, but he was the last person he wanted to see just now. An unheralded visit probably meant work in the offing, his list was pretty full, but it was always difficult to disoblige a friend. Come to think of it, that was why Geoffrey was here in person, instead of sending the papers into chambers in the usual way. 'I saw his car outside,' he added, making for the staircase. Gibbs, as usual, had very effectively aroused a quite illogical feeling of guilt. 'Is my uncle in yet?'

'Not yet, Mr Maitland.' Now his tone seemed to reprove a lack of attention to duty, which brought some men home before others, more conscientious. Antony said, 'Thank you,' again, for want of anything better, and started up the stairs two at a time.

Jenny came into the hall while he was still divesting himself of his overcoat. 'Geoffrey's here,' she said in a neutral sort of tone, as though uncertain of his reaction. Her husband smiled at her.

'So Gibbs told me. Is he staying for dinner?'

'He says Joan's expecting him. But he wanted to talk to you.' They went together into the living-room, which was large and a trifle shabby. Having been furnished in a rather makeshift way when shopping was difficult in the early post-war years, nothing matched anything else except the two wing chairs on either side of the fire-place. But it was undeniably comfortable, and pleasantly warm on that cold January night, and it had an air of tranquillity about it that was solely due to Jenny's presence, and that Antony always liked to savour in the moment of homecoming.

That evening there was no time to do so. Geoffrey Horton, on his feet in front of the fire, said without preamble, 'So you've got here at last.'

Maitland was making for the writing-table where a tray was set out. 'You mustn't be impatient, Geoffrey,' he said reprovingly. 'Are you supplied? Well then, sit down and tell me all about it.'

Jenny had gone back to her favourite place on the sofa. Geoffrey took the chair that was reserved for Sir Nicholas on his frequent visits. Antony put his glass on the mantelpiece, moved a little out of the direct line of the fire, and said, 'Come now,' in an encouraging way, as though he were the one who had been kept waiting, and not his friend.

'I've got a case for you,' said Geoffrey.

'Something told me you were going to say that.'

'Not – not an easy one,' Geoffrey continued, elaborating unnecessarily.

'You didn't have to tell me that either,' said Maitland rather sharply. 'When you start badgering me at home—'

Horton smiled at him apologetically. 'Well, I know you don't feel like talking shop at this hour,' he said. 'You might find it interesting, for all that.'

'I might,' said Antony cordially. Horton, who knew him very well, looked alarmed.

'You can at least listen,' he protested.

'What else am I to do?' Maitland retrieved his glass

11

and sipped his sherry thoughtfully. 'Come to the point, Geoffrey,' he urged, 'there's a good chap.'

'It's a case of murder,' said Horton, still not abandoning his defensive pose.

Antony sighed. 'Your client, I suppose, being the murderer,' he said.

'Well ... I think so.'

'I see. He says he's innocent, but you're not so sure.'

'Exactly. No, I'm misleading you, I am sure ... about the guilty part, I mean. But it isn't a man, it's a woman ... Ellen Gray.'

'A name that conjures up a picture of all the old-fashioned virtues.'

'I wouldn't exactly say—'

'What would you say, for heaven's sake? All this beating about the bush, Geoffrey. You're making me fear the worst.'

'She's twenty-seven. A nice girl – well then, young woman, if you prefer it – but not exactly ... certainly not old-fashioned.'

'It isn't a matter of what I prefer, it's a matter of accuracy,' said Antony maddeningly. He was a tall man, with dark hair and a thin, intelligent face, and a humorous look that just now was becoming very marked. 'Are you trying to break it to me that she's a modern, liberated woman?'

'Not that either. Though, come to think of it, I suppose I don't know her well enough to say. She's very good looking, very well turned out—'

'And in prison, awaiting trial.'

'That's right.'

'Stop sounding so doubtful, then, and tell me what's troubling you.'

'It's the background to the case. You may not like it,' Geoffrey warned.

'Since you're obviously determined to tell me, you may as well get it over with.'

'Her father was convicted of murdering his wife and her lover nineteen, nearly twenty, years ago, and died in prison in 1956,' said Geoffrey baldly.

'I see. Is the contention then that murder runs in the family?'

'No, of course not. But the alleged motive springs from that old case.' Horton sounded more confident now.

'As she can only have been a child at the time—'

'Eight years old.'

'—it's a little difficult to understand how that can be so.'

'Well,' said Geoffrey again, and pulled himself up on the word. 'Apparently she was devoted to her father, but she accepted the verdict like anybody else until just recently.'

'When we first met, Geoffrey – was it twelve years ago? – it was over a very similar case.'

'I was hoping you wouldn't remember that,' said Horton frankly.

'I don't quite see—'

'It upset you pretty much at the time.'

'So it did.' There was something in his tone again that made the other man uneasy. Horton glanced at Jenny, and met a clear, candid look, and wondered what she was really thinking. But Antony was speaking, he hadn't time to pursue the thought. 'Has Miss Gray ... or is she married?'

'No.'

'Was she also brought up to be continually reminded of her unfortunate heritage?' His glass was empty now, and he put it back on the mantelpiece. Jenny got up quietly, a moment later, and refilled it, and Geoffrey's, and her own.

'Nothing like that,' said Geoffrey, rather hurriedly,

13

as if he didn't want an unpleasant notion to have time to take root. 'The two cases don't really have so very much in common, as you'll see when you've heard a little more. Miss Gray was brought up by a cousin of her mother's, a Doctor Clive and his wife. I haven't seen them yet, but from what she tells me they sound to be normal, kindly people, very much concerned to allow her to forget.'

'But you say that recently something sparked off her interest again.'

'She got engaged. Or, to be accurate, she says it isn't official. But she wanted to be married – she told the police all this when first they interviewed her – and I suppose she thought about the possibility of having children and all that, so she began to enquire into the circumstances of her father's case with the result that she convinced herself he was innocent.'

'That should have settled her doubts once and for all, shouldn't it?'

'In a way it did. But unfortunately she also learned some of the facts about her father's trial and the dead man – the man she's accused of murdering – was one of the principal witnesses against him.'

'You're telling me they're citing revenge as a motive. That sounds a bit far fetched.'

'You haven't talked to Ellen. Still, of course, that isn't all they've got against her.'

'So I suppose.' The fire was burning up vigorously now, it must have been mended just before he came in, and he shifted his position a little and then, changing his mind, took his glass and went to sit in the other wing chair, the twin to the one that his visitor was occupying. 'Tell me the worst,' he said.

'The dead man's name was John Wilcox. He was a stockbroker. Married, two children in their teens. They had a flat in Bayswater; I should say, "have", Mrs Wilcox and the children are still there.'

'Was the dead man known to Miss Gray before she came across his name in the account of the trial?'

'Oh, yes, very well known. She told me she used to call him "uncle" when she was younger. But she's a bit of a fanatic on the subject of her father's innocence now. You'll see! So she went storming round to the Bayswater flat to have it out with Wilcox. Mrs Wilcox was out, and the young people were in the dining-room playing table tennis. They heard a sound "like a car backfiring", without taking any immediate notice of it; then one of them – the girl – got uneasy, thought it had sounded too loud, something like that, and went across the hall into the drawing-room. She found her father dead, lying back in the chair he usually occupied, as if he'd got up to greet a visitor and been shot before he had time to cry out or take any evasive action. Ellen Gray was standing behind the chair that is opposite the fireplace – I've got a plan that I'll send you – and a gun, subsequently proved to be the one that had killed him, was lying on the seat of the chair.'

'As if it had dropped from her nerveless hand,' said Maitland sardonically. And then, more sharply, 'Finger-prints?'

'All present and correct.'

'That makes things difficult, doesn't it? Who is the investigating officer?'

'Detective Inspector Conway,' said Horton, without any expression in his voice.

'Oh, lord!'

'It doesn't really matter.'

'No, not really!' The mockery in Maitland's tone was a little too pronounced for comfort, but he went on immediately, without waiting for the other man to comment. 'What is your client's story? And, incidentally, did either of the children hear her arrive?'

'No, she had a key because she used to baby-sit for them when they were younger.'

'You did say I was going to find this interesting, didn't you?'

'A challenge,' said Geoffrey, and grinned.

'Heaven and earth! But you were going to tell me what Miss Gray has to say for herself.'

'She'd just arrived. A fearful shock, of course, but she could see it was quite useless to try to do anything for him. The gun – a Mauser automatic pistol – was lying on the floor near the door, and she was in a kind of daze when she picked it up and then dropped it on to the seat of the chair where it was found.'

'Did either of the children ... what are their names, anyway? There must be some way of distinguishing them.'

'Barbara and Roy. What about them?'

'Did either of them remember how long it was since they heard what must be presumed to have been the shot?'

'Barbara said it was quite five minutes. Roy thinks it was only a few seconds before Barbara broke off their game and went to investigate.'

'A bit of a discrepancy there, but nothing Counsel for the Prosecution can't gloss over if he wants.'

'Must you take the gloomiest view?' Horton demanded. 'I should have thought that would give you a lever, at least.'

'My dear Geoffrey, I need more than that.'

'That's why I thought—'

'I know, I know. But you'd better spell it out for me. I take it that all this happened recently, and that Miss Gray was arrested as soon as the police came on the scene.'

'As soon as she'd handed them her motive on a platter.

16

The murder was back in November. Wednesday, the eleventh.'

'Then ... look here, when does the trial come on, Geoffrey?'

'Early in this session.'

'When?' said Antony inexorably.

'Next week most likely. Halloran's got the prosecution, and it's on Carruthers's list.'

'I see. Or do I? Why the hell have you left it all this time?'

'Because Mallory wasn't exactly encouraging when I spoke to him.' (Old Mr Mallory was Sir Nicholas's clerk.) 'And,' continued Geoffrey, making a virtue of necessity, 'I didn't think it was exactly in your line.'

'Then why approach me now, at this late date?'

'Kevin O'Brien's having an emergency appendectomy,' said Horton, with engaging frankness. Antony began to laugh.

'My list's still full,' he said.

'But—'

'For old times' sake I am to rearrange it, over-rule Mallory ... which won't make me popular, let me remind you.'

'A lot you care for that.'

'I do care, as a matter of fact. He will probably accept all the dullest cases he can find for me next session. Still—'

'You'll do it!'

'I suppose I must.'

Horton's sigh of relief showed how little he had thought the result of his request a foregone conclusion. 'I shall want to see the girl,' said Maitland warningly, as the other man began to express his gratitude.

'I don't see why,' said Geoffrey, breaking off what he had been saying. 'It's quite straightforward ... all in the brief.'

'I'm sure it is. All the same—'

'It might be a good idea, at that. Perhaps you can persuade her to be sensible.'

'What, in your view, does that entail?'

'Pleading guilty, and trying to get away with "diminished responsibility". It's the best hope we have.'

'I see. Well, who lives may learn. I may not agree with you, you know.'

'You will.' Geoffrey was in no doubt about it. Now, with an air of duty well done, he sat back comfortably in his chair and began to sip the sherry which had been standing neglected at his elbow.

Maitland, relaxed in his turn, had a different cause for self-congratulation. It was nothing out of the ordinary – he honestly thought that! – nothing to worry about, nothing to disturb his peace of mind except perhaps the unpleasantness of having to interview the prisoner. But that was before he met Ellen Gray.

MONDAY, 18th January

I

Jenny was silent as she gave him his breakfast, respecting his mood. As always, the prospect of prison visiting lay on his spirits like a pall. Monday morning, too. But he'd promised himself that as soon as opportunity offered he would go with Geoffrey to see his client, and here was a morning that, although it could profitably have been used for other things, wasn't inextricably tied up.

He was lingering over his second cup of coffee when Horton arrived. Geoffrey was cheerful this morning – as well he might be, thought Antony a little sourly – and quite ready to dawdle a little. In fact, it was Maitland himself who finally proposed that they should get on with it, much against his inclination. Having found a convenient parking space in the square, Horton wasn't inclined to give it up again; so they walked round the corner into Avery Street and picked up a taxi outside the hotel.

It was a pleasant morning for January, cold but bright. Geoffrey discoursed determinedly upon his search for a new car – a subject which would have amused Jenny more than it did her husband – and did not seem to notice his companion's taciturnity. But he did say, though still good-humouredly, as he paid off the cab outside the prison, 'It won't be as bad as all that, Antony. She's not likely to throw a fit of hysterics, or anything like that.'

That wasn't what Maitland was afraid of. He hated prisons, the institutional smell of them, the rattle of keys and – worst of all – the closing of doors that sounded as though they would never open again. And all this predisposed him to sympathise with the prisoner, whoever he or she might be, and that was the last emotion he wanted to experience. Apart from the fact that such sympathy had more than once been misplaced, he could deal with the matter so much more efficiently – or so he thought – on a purely objective plane.

He hadn't obtained any very clear impression of Ellen Gray from what Geoffrey had told him; certainly nothing the solicitor had said had prepared him for a spectacularly good-looking young woman, and it took him a moment to absorb this fact before he realised that she was nervous, and taking some pains to hide it; and also that there was something hostile in the look she gave him as the introductions were effected. Well, if she didn't like him, that might be all to the good.

He had plenty of opportunity to study her as they seated themselves at the long, rather dusty table, with himself at one end and the girl at the other, and Horton somewhere between them, not unlike the umpire at a tennis match. Geoffrey was proceeding smoothly with his opening remarks; he was a great one for the courtesies, even – perhaps particularly – in so unconventional a situation as this. But there was no need to listen to him, Maitland knew it all by heart. So he looked at the prisoner instead.

Ellen Gray was tallish for a woman, about two inches taller than Jenny he had noted as she came into the room. Her hair was the colour that has been described as 'dark mouse', but there were golden lights in it, even in that bleak room where the sun probably never penetrated. It was thick, and waved almost to her shoulders, and still looked beautifully groomed; so that he thought again of Jenny, brushing steadily at her brown curls, because surely that was the only beauty treatment that would be available here. For the rest, Ellen's eyes were a clear hazel, her nose a little too small and her mouth a little too wide for real beauty, but combined with a creamy complexion the overall effect was pretty stunning. He thought – but there was more amusement in it than complaining – that Geoffrey should have warned him. There were problems in having a beauty for a client. Her looks might arouse sympathy, but were far more likely to provoke an unrecognised antagonism.

He became aware that Geoffrey had finished speaking and was looking at him hopefully. But before he could say anything Ellen spoke. She had a nice voice, clear but not too assertive. There was a trace of a quiver in it, which wasn't surprising, and still that unexpected, unexplained hostility. 'I've already told Mr Horton everything I know,' she said.

'I wonder.'

'Of course I have! I'd be a fool if I hadn't.'

'You'll have to forgive me, Miss Gray. I have a weakness for hearing things for myself.'

'And for weighing up your clients before you take them on. I've heard of you, Mr Maitland.'

She couldn't have said anything to antagonise him more quickly. He said, 'I don't know quite what you mean by that. I've accepted the brief, as Mr Horton told you.'

'Yes, but there's more to it than that. If you think I'm telling the truth you'll try to help me. Otherwise—'

'I shall do my best for you, in either event.' He said that rather sharply, and she flushed, but went on doggedly,

'All the same, you're here to judge me.'

'Nothing of the kind.' But how much truth was there in the accusation? 'I'm not likely to forget that's the

21

jury's job, Miss Gray. I don't think you should forget it either. And I must point out that time hardly permits me to indulge in what my uncle calls "meddling" in your affairs.'

'Beyond the call of duty,' she said quickly. There was an edge of sarcasm to her voice, and this time he smiled at her with open amusement.

'Exactly,' he agreed. 'But, leaving all that aside, I must have some facts to work on. You do see that?'

'I suppose so,' she said grudgingly. He thought perhaps she wasn't used to being laughed at.

'Then you'll answer my questions?'

'As far as I can. I may as well tell you straight away, there are a lot of things I don't know the answer to. Mr Horton will tell you.'

'Yes, but ... forget Mr Horton for a moment. He won't be hurt, I promise you, and he won't be bored if you repeat yourself.'

'Very well.' She was sitting with her hands clasped on the table in front of her, and now he saw the skin whiten as her fingers gripped more tightly. 'What do you want to know?'

'Tell me first about what happened when you were eight years old.'

'No!'

'Miss Gray, you agreed—'

'That can't be relevant,' she said less vehemently; making an obvious effort, in fact, to sound reasonable.

'At this stage, none of us can say what's relevant.' No use emphasising at this point that a knowledge of the old case would be essential if they wanted to plead 'diminished responsibility'. She had enough to worry about, poor girl, without that. All the same, he half expected further argument, and was both surprised and relieved when she said again, 'Very well.' But this time she moved her hands so that they were hidden in her lap.

'Tell me then, what you remember. About the kind of life you led, first of all.'

'We lived, my mother and I, in one of the blocks of flats near Putney Heath.' She started readily enough, but then went on more hesitantly. 'They were built just before the war, and were quite luxurious, I suppose. My mother had some money from her father. None of my grandparents was living, which was unusual – wasn't it? – seeing how young my parents were at the time.'

'How young?'

'My father was nearly thirty, and my mother three years younger. They'd been married at what was an early age then.'

'I see. Go on with your story,' he added encouragingly.

'It seems so—'

'You're doing splendidly,' he told her. She started up again obediently enough, but she sounded doubtful.

'As long as I remembered there'd been the war, with my father away, but now it was over – the only difference there seemed to be really was that there weren't any more bombs – and he ought to have been coming home. Even I understood that, but mother would never talk about it. It was only later that I knew he had been missing.'

'Just a moment. Your father's name—'

'Edward. My mother was Madeleine.'

'He was in the army?'

'Yes. As long as I remembered,' she said again. 'But he was always a very special person to me, because wonderful things happened when he came home on leave. I wasn't even frightened of the air raids when he was there. But it seemed an awfully long time since I'd seen him.'

'What was his peacetime occupation?'

'He was an architect. That's why—' She broke off there and added, but without any apology in her tone,

23

'But I'm getting ahead of my story.'

'Never mind. What were you going to say?'

'Just that it was why I looked for a job in an architect's office after I left school.'

'You're engaged to the man you worked for, aren't you?'

'Not engaged. It hadn't got as far as that. There were things I wanted to know first.'

'I see. Back to 1945, Miss Gray.'

'I don't know what else you want to know.'

'Your mother's friends—'

'Are you going to judge her too?' she asked. There was some bitterness in her tone, and this time he reacted defensively.

'I hoped I had made it clear to you—'

'I know what you said, Mr Maitland.'

'Then—'

'It really is important, Miss Gray,' Geoffrey Horton put in.

'I must take your word for it.' She still sounded grudging. 'My mother's friends? There were so many of them. I mean, they were friends of both my mother and father, but as far as the men were concerned their leaves didn't often coincide.'

Maitland was feeling in his pocket, and produced presently a rather dishevelled envelope. 'If you could be a little more specific,' he said.

'I can only remember the names of those I still know today. First there were Uncle William and Aunt Alison. They're cousins really, he was my mother's first cousin, and we saw more of them than of anybody else because he wasn't in the Forces and they lived quite near. He's a doctor ... well, so is Aunt Alison, but she doesn't practise now.'

'That's Doctor Clive, who adopted you after your parents' death.'

24

'Yes. At least, my father wasn't dead then, you know.'

'I know.' He sounded sympathetic, and Horton gave him an uneasy look.

'Everybody does.'

'I think you're exaggerating. Or perhaps most of your uncle's friends were your parents' friends too.'

'The ones I was going to tell you about.'

'Then that accounts for it, doesn't it?'

'Perhaps it does. But nobody ever reminded me, in fact they were all awfully careful not to.'

'I'm glad of that. Just their names will do for now.'

'Martin and Dorothy Roydon.' She paused while he wrote that down. 'Fred Tate and his wife Mathilda. John and Frances Wilcox.' She stumbled a little over the words. 'It's John I'm supposed to have killed.'

'Time enough for that later.'

'Yes, but I don't understand—' She thought better of that and went on with a valiant attempt at self-possession. 'I used to call them all Aunt and Uncle, of course, but I gave that up ages ago.'

'And they were your parents' closest friends.'

'Yes ... no, I'm misleading you. Martin and Fred didn't marry until after the war, so I didn't know their wives until I was living with Uncle William.'

Maitland carefully drew circles round the two names, Dorothy and Mathilda. 'There's one name missing from the list, you know.' He did not raise his eyes until he had asked the question, but then his look startled her by being unexpectedly keen, and she stammered a little over her reply.

'You mean Uncle M-michael. Michael Foster.'

'Yes.'

'I don't see why—'

'Bear with me.' He smiled at her suddenly. 'We're really not wasting time.'

'If you say so. He was a friend of my father's too.'

'Can you remember his occupation?'

'I know it now, because I asked Uncle William about him. He was a bank clerk, and he wasn't in the Forces because of something wrong with his heart, so we saw more of him than of the others.'

'We? You and your mother?'

'That's what I meant.' She sounded belligerent about it, and he hastened to reassure her.

'I'm sorry, really I am. I know he's the man your father's accused of killing, but I don't suppose at that age you noticed anything out of the ordinary in his friendship with your mother.'

'No, I didn't. And I don't believe now that there was.'

'I see.' He sounded thoughtful, but his next question put her back on course again, ignoring the possible diversion. 'Do you remember the night of the tragedy?'

'I don't remember anything at all about it. I was asleep.'

'And afterwards?'

'Uncle William came the next morning and took me away. He told me my mother was dead, but he let me think my father was still away with the army. Only later on I heard things, and when I asked him he told me the truth. What he thought was the truth, at least.'

Again he ignored the implication. 'You really remember nothing of what happened?'

'Nothing at all.'

'All right then, let's get to the part you want to tell me. What made you decide, after all these years, that your father was innocent?'

She gave him a smile then, and it lighted up her face to real beauty. 'Of course I want to tell you,' she said. 'You've got an open mind, Mr Maitland. You may even agree with me.'

'Try me.' In spite of her seeming eagerness she did not respond immediately, and after a moment he added encouragingly, 'Did you start to look at the evidence because you wanted to be married?'

'Not really. I mean when I discovered what I did naturally I wanted to go on with it for that reason. But I never thought about it until I came across a poem my mother had written, a fragment really, scribbled on the fly-leaf of her copy of Palgrave's *Golden Treasury*.'

'That sounds intriguing.'

'To explain I'll have to remind you that my father was "missing, believed killed" and came home unexpectedly. The poem could only have been written after Mother heard about that, and it showed quite clearly that she loved him. So it couldn't have been true to say that there was anything between her and Michael Foster.'

'There is always the question – forgive me – of how long it was since your mother had had the news.'

'Only six months! She couldn't have changed her mind in so short a time.'

'It sounds unlikely, certainly. Do you remember the poem?'

'Not properly. Aunt Alison would get the book for you though. It's in my bedroom with some others that were my parents', only we didn't use Palgrave at school, so I'd never happened to look in it. But, Mr Maitland, it means there was no cause for my father to be jealous. He wouldn't have shot them both if he'd just found them sitting together.'

'That's a point you can enlighten me on, Geoffrey. Where were they found?'

'In the living-room. The prosecution maintained there had been some conversation, in the course of which the "true situation" revealed itself.'

'And what was the defence?'

'Edward Gray said that he'd found them both dead.' Horton was readier with his facts than his client had been. 'There was a gun on the floor – a target pistol he'd owned since before the war – and he said he'd left it at home, unloaded, in the top drawer of the bureau that stood just inside the living-room door. But John Wilcox gave evidence that Edward had told him he was taking it with him. He'd always been interested in target shooting, and that particular weapon "felt right in his hand".'

'It was John's evidence that convicted him really,' said Ellen. 'At least, that's what I thought when Uncle William told me of it.'

'If the gun was left at home, unloaded, there's the question of ammunition.'

'That was in the drawer too, or so my father said.'

'Fingerprints?' He turned to Geoffrey again, questioningly.

'The gun had been wiped clean. The prosecution contended that he did that himself, before he phoned for the police. There was a discrepancy in time that tended to support that theory. Wilcox saw him go into the block of flats at eight-fifteen, and the phone call was received at the local police station at eight thirty-five.'

'You see what I mean,' said Ellen. 'John might have been his enemy, instead of one of his closest friends.'

'I don't think that follows, you know.'

'I do!'

'So it seems. We should be obliged to you – Mr Horton and I – if you could contrive to forget that particular grievance.'

'I suppose you mean, I was a fool to tell the police. But I had to, Mr Maitland. They asked me what I was doing at John's, and that was the reason I'd gone to see him. So what else could I say?'

'There are times when it is profitable to say nothing at all. But it can't be helped now.' He turned to Geoffrey again. 'What did Edward Gray have to say to that?'

'That he was stunned by what he found. That it took

him that time to collect his wits.'

'Well, there's this much in his favour, it wouldn't have taken him twenty minutes to wipe the gun clean. There's still some time to be accounted for, and his version will do as well as another.'

'I suppose he might have fired the shots, and then been horrified by what he had done.'

'You can't have it both ways, Geoffrey. According to the prosecution he was at least calm enough to wipe the gun clear of fingerprints.'

'You're beginning to believe me, Mr Maitland,' said Ellen eagerly, and he turned to her smiling a little.

'Not so fast, Miss Gray, not so fast. We've still a long way to go. And most likely, as you said, it has no relevance.'

'No, I don't think it has. But I do wish I could convince you.'

'It's more important to convince the jury of your innocence, if that's what you want to do.'

'Of course it is.'

'Well, we shan't do it if you continue to display such open animosity towards the dead man.'

'I don't think I'm a very good liar.'

'You needn't lie, but at least you could suppress the truth,' he said rather tartly. Geoffrey gave a sigh, which might have been of relief, and sat back in his chair again.

Unexpectedly, Ellen was smiling. 'I'll do my best,' she said. Maitland didn't trust her sudden submissiveness an inch, and said so.

'I imagine you'll continue to do just as you please,' he said. 'So we may as well go on to the next question. What happened the day John Wilcox died?'

'But surely Mr Horton told you?'

'I want to hear it for myself. Remember?'

'Yes.' It was her turn to sigh, not at all resignedly. 'I wanted to see John, I told you that.'

'Just a moment. How did that come about, at precisely that time?'

'I cornered Uncle William before dinner. For once he was in time to have a drink with us. He told me about the trial.'

'This seems as good a time as any to ask, how did John Wilcox come to see your father on his way home?'

'He was coming to see us. When he met my father he said he wouldn't spoil the surprise, nobody had known he was coming home you see. So my father went in alone.'

'Back to the present. You were talking to Doctor Clive.'

'Yes, it wasn't easy to get him to talk, but after a while he did. That was the first I had heard of John's evidence, you see. And I was angry. It sounded like deliberate spite.'

'You'd already made up your mind your father was innocent?'

'The poem made me sure of that. He had no motive.'

'Have you another candidate for the part of first murderer?'

'At that time I'd hardly thought about it. But since I came here I've wondered if perhaps John—'

'Heaven and earth! Are you deliberately trying to make things sound worse than they are?' enquired Antony explosively.

'If I can't tell *you* what I think—'

'Yes, of course. It's highly desirable that you should. But nobody else. Mr Horton will tell you that too.'

'I certainly will,' Geoffrey agreed with feeling. 'Unless, of course—' But Ellen wasn't listening to him.

'Anyway, it's quite a reasonable thought,' she said. 'He might have been leaving when he met my father, at the very least he was there that night.'

'Did Edward Gray say that?'

'No, he said they met in the street. Even so—'

'In the absence of any other candidates, perhaps,' said Maitland doubtfully. 'There's one thing that puzzles me, Miss Gray. How did it come about that you didn't hear anything that night? You can't have been long in bed.'

'I had a cold. Mother put me to bed early, and gave me some cough syrup. That always made me drowsy, I didn't even hear my father come in.'

'Or anybody else, I suppose?'

'I'd have told you – well, I'd have told Uncle Will long since – if I had.'

'It's more likely that you'd have heard the shots.'

'But I didn't.'

'No. I suppose they may have disturbed your dreams, and afterwards you wouldn't remember it,' said Antony thoughtfully. 'But we'd better get back to the present. What Doctor Clive told you made you angry—'

'I didn't wait for dinner. I couldn't have eaten any. I left the house about half past seven.'

'That's in Roehampton Lane?'

'Yes, not far from the village.'

'You still live there with your uncle and aunt?'

'Yes. I've sometimes thought I'd like to be on my own, but it didn't seem fair to leave them when they wanted me to stay, after they'd been so good to me.'

'And from Roehampton you had to get to—?'

'Bayswater. The Wilcoxes have a flat there, an enormous place with huge rooms, but more comfortable than grand really.'

'How long did the journey take you?'

'I'm sorry, I never noticed. I've thought and thought about this, Mr Maitland, because Mr Horton said it was important, but I can't remember how long it took me to get a bus, or how much traffic there was on the way, or anything. I got off in Knightsbridge and walked across the park, and I've not timed myself so I don't know how

31

long that took either. By the time I looked at my watch again it was past nine o'clock, and the police had already arrived and herded us into the dining-room until they were ready to question us.'

'You, and Barbara, and Roy. Did they suspect you too?'

'Yes, they did. That hurt, Mr Maitland, though I suppose it was natural in the circumstances.'

'Perhaps it was. Let's see now. You walked across the park, and didn't notice your time of arrival. Is it an upstairs flat?'

'Yes. Well, it isn't a flat at all really, though they always call it that. It's half a house, and the bedrooms are on the top floor, what must have been the servants' rooms originally.'

'You arrived. Did you need two keys to get in?'

'I did. There's a downstairs door, to which both tenants have keys, and then their own front door at the top of the stairs.'

'I see. Tell me what happened.'

'I went in—'

'Could you hear Barbara and Roy playing table tennis?'

'No, but I could hear their voices from the dining-room. I think, from what they told the police, that must have been when they were discussing what they had heard. So I went straight to the drawing-room.'

'Knowing that Wilcox would be there, and alone?'

'I have to say no to both those things, though I admit it never occurred to me that he might not be at home. I suppose if I'd thought about it I'd have expected Frances to be with him, but I didn't think it out and even if I had done I shouldn't have cared.'

'Frances. Is that Mrs Wilcox?'

'Yes. They were married during the war, I think. She knew my parents.'

32

Maitland was underlining the name Frances on his envelope. When he had finished he looked up and said quietly, 'You were telling me what you found in the drawing-room.'

'I'd much rather not.'

'I dare say. You must, however. Mr Horton will tell you—'

'Yes, I suppose he will agree with you,' she said, without, however, any animosity in her tone, only a hint of dryness. 'I went in, and I stopped short in the doorway, because there was John, in his usual chair ... that's the one on the right as you face the fireplace. And his jacket had fallen open and there was blood on his shirt. I'm not used to death, but I was in no doubt at all that he was dead.'

'He'd been shot through the heart, and must have died as nearly instantly as makes no matter,' Horton put in.

'I see.' Maitland sounded thoughtful. 'Have you ever fired a Mauser automatic, Miss Gray?'

'No, but I have done some target shooting. It was something I always wanted to try, because of it being a hobby of my father, I suppose. There's a range in East Sheen, and when I told Stephen about it he took me several times.'

'You do make things difficult, don't you? How did you get on?'

'Fairly well.'

'If Stephen ... what's his name, by the way?'

'Langland. Stephen Langland. I work for him.'

Maitland wrote that down too, taking his time. 'Is he the man you're going to marry?' he asked.

'There's nothing settled about that.'

'Yes, I'm sorry. You've told me that once already, haven't you?' he said, answering her tone rather than the words. 'I was going to say, if Mr Langland can give evidence that you're not a crack shot that should help matters a little.' Ellen made no reply to that, and for the moment her eyes did not meet his. So he went on, after the silence had lengthened a little, 'What did you do after you had decided that John Wilcox was dead?'

'I saw the gun. It was right in front of the door, just a foot or so into the room. And I picked it up.' She hesitated, and then added in rather a belligerent tone, 'Well, I know it was stupid, but I honestly never thought about it then. And I went forward into the room, to look at John more closely, and I suppose I must have dropped the gun in the chair where the police found it, but I don't remember that at all. And then Roy and Barbara came in.'

'I imagine there must have been quite a scene.'

'I tried to keep them out, of course, and succeeded to some extent with Barbara. But there was no doing anything with Roy, and I must admit he was the calmest of the three of us. It was he who called the police.'

'How long do you think it was between your going into the drawing-room and the two young people following you?'

'A matter of moments, I think. I hesitated in the doorway, and then went forward, and almost immediately they were there.'

'That's quite an important point, you know. If you were in shock—'

'I ... yes, I was shocked, of course, or I wouldn't have picked up the gun. But I'm sure it was no time at all before they were there.'

'How old are they, Barbara and Roy?'

'Barbara's sixteen and Roy's fourteen.'

'Now we come to another important point. Did you see anyone leaving the flat as you went in?'

'No.'

'Or driving away, or walking away down the street?'

34

'If I had, don't you think I'd have told Mr Horton?' Her tone was challenging, but there was something about it that made him uneasy.

'I should have expected you to, certainly. But you haven't answered my question.'

'No ... no!'

'I'm sorry, Miss Gray.' He didn't sound it. 'You feel this has been going on long enough, don't you? Would it upset you very much to know we've only scratched the surface?'

'Mr Horton warned me,' she said, 'but I didn't know ... I didn't realise—'

'One question after another. I'm really sorry,' he said again. 'But now I'm afraid we've got to go back to the beginning. First, though, there's the question of your plea.'

'I suppose you're going to tell me you agree with Mr Horton about that.'

'I'm afraid I do.'

'My father wouldn't compromise his principles by pleading Guilty, though he might have got off quite lightly if he had done.'

Maitland chose to ignore that. 'If you agree – and I do assure you I think it would be the best thing – the more you have to say about your father's case the better, and we shall be calling you to give evidence. Otherwise, as I said before, the more you can suppress your feelings the better.'

'I didn't kill John, and I won't say I did. But of course I'll give evidence. How will anybody know the truth if I don't?'

'To put you on the witness stand would be to lay you open to Halloran's cross-examination. If you were going to plead Guilty that would be all to the good; I think – I'm being frank with you – that the jury would feel you were so misguided as to come under the protection of that useful phrase "diminished responsibility". But if you insist on a straight Not Guilty plea, all that *must* be kept from the jury.'

'What do you mean, a "straight" plea?'

'I've been talking about your pleading Guilty, but actually it would be "Not Guilty by reason of diminished responsibility".'

'That doesn't make any difference.' She paused there, eyeing him again in rather a hostile way. 'So you don't believe me about my father?'

'Miss Gray, I've tried to explain to you, what I believe doesn't matter.'

'It does to me. I'd just like to feel that someone—'

'I'm sorry.' This time he sounded sincere. 'We'll come back to this, Miss Gray, we'll have to. But now I want you to tell me again exactly what happened – in greater detail this time – on the day John Wilcox was killed.'

II

'I must admit I hoped you'd have more luck with her,' said Geoffrey as they left the prison some time later. 'Of all the stubborn—'

'You mustn't blame her too much for that. She's a convert to the idea of her father's innocence, and all the more fierce about it because she doubted it for so long.'

'I don't see what that has to do with it.'

'He pleaded Not Guilty, not "compromising his principles" ... I bet she thought that phrase up beforehand. So she will follow his example.'

'At least,' said Horton, looking on the bright side, 'she agreed to stay out of the witness box. But the police have her statement, you know. If they can get that introduced—'

'Let's worry about that later on. I wish she'd taken our

advice, Geoffrey, but you can't help admiring the stand she's making.'

'Yes, I thought that was how you felt about it.'

'How do you make that out?' asked Maitland, stopping dead in his tracks.

'Because I've never heard you speak sharply to a client with whom you weren't to some degree in sympathy.'

'I find that disconcerting,' said Antony, amused. He began to walk on again. 'Heaven preserve us from our friends.'

'In fact, I almost believed at one point that you thought she was innocent.'

'No, that's going too far. She'd rehearsed her story well though, you have to admit that. It was only when she got to the part she hadn't rehearsed that the lies showed through.'

'I thought she sounded completely candid throughout.'

'Not all the time.'

'You're splitting hairs, Antony.'

'Wait and see.'

'What do you want to do now?'

'We must see what Doctor and Mrs Clive have to say for themselves, since you say that neither of them is being called by the prosecution. No, I haven't got it right, have I? Miss Gray said they are both doctors.'

'But Aunt Alison no longer practises,' Horton reminded him. 'It would be less confusing to stick to Mrs Clive for her.'

'What do you suppose would be a good time to catch them?'

'I thought perhaps ... now.'

'Surely the good doctor will be in surgery, or on his rounds, or something.'

'No, he promised to turn his patients over to his partner this morning.'

'Do I detect that I'm being managed? What a good wife you'd have made for somebody, Geoffrey. Quite up to Mrs Beeton's specifications.'

'Well, you said you wanted to see them,' said Horton reasonably. 'I only anticipated your wishes by a little.'

'Very well then. If that's an empty cab, we'll take it.' He halted again, waving energetically. 'You really ought to have brought the car with you, Geoffrey. This is going to cost the earth.'

III

Doctor William Clive was a large, shaggy man, and Antony took to him instantly. Given the tragic circumstances in which an eight-year-old girl had found herself nineteen years ago, there could have been, he thought, no kinder guardian. Doctor Clive received them in the drawing-room of the house in Roehampton Lane, and offered at once to fetch his wife. 'We do want to see her,' Geoffrey assured him. 'But perhaps it will be as well for us to have a word or two with you first.'

'Yes, indeed. All this has upset her, as you can imagine.' He looked appraisingly from one of them to the other. 'And you're trying to help our poor Ellen.'

'If we can.'

'Have you seen her yet?'

'We came here from the prison.'

'How is she then?' The question came eagerly, and Antony, to whom it seemed to be addressed, hesitated a moment before replying.

'I should say very well, given the circumstances,' he said, and smiled, trying to lighten the doctor's anxiety. 'In fact, I have seldom had a more self-possessed client.'

'Yes, I can imagine that.' He smiled too, reminiscently, and there seemed to be some pride in the way he

38

spoke. 'But I haven't seen her since that night, when she left the house in anger. Does she . . . has she told you—?'

'She says Wilcox was dead when she arrived.'

'Thank God for that! You will forgive me, but I have been so anxious. It was difficult to know what to believe.'

'And now you do?' Maitland's tone was more gentle than the words, but the doctor took him up sharply.

'If Ellen says she is innocent, there is no question about it at all.' Horton muttered something indistinguishable, but Antony just stood looking gravely at the speaker, so that William Clive added, more anxious now than annoyed, 'That is how she will plead?'

'Certainly.'

'I ask because of something Martin said.'

'What was that, doctor?'

'That it might be open to her to plead guilty to a reduced charge.'

'That is something about which we can only advise Miss Gray, we have to accept her decision. This Martin you speak of—?'

'Martin Roydon, a very old friend.'

'Is he a lawyer?'

'No, a chartered accountant. Chief Accountant of Willoughby's. But I'm keeping you standing, this thing has got me so confused. Please sit down.'

There was a pause while they seated themselves. Maitland took the opportunity of looking round the room, and was puzzled by his reaction. With Doctor Clive he had been conscious of an instant rapport, even before a word was spoken. But with the room it was another story. Comfortably, even luxuriously furnished, old-fashioned in a nice sort of way, the kind of place that should have set you immediately at ease. Only it didn't. There was an atmosphere . . . as if it had seen too much sorrow, he thought, but that was fanciful. A weak-minded reaction to what he knew of Ellen Gray.

Doctor Clive was talking. Something about being glad of the opportunity to speak to them. 'You will be able to tell me, Mr Maitland, as Mr Horton could not when I spoke to him previously, what chance Ellen has.'

'I'm afraid I'm as much in the dark as he is. But I think you should understand that the circumstances in which she was found – in the room with the dead man, with her fingerprints on the gun – create a strong presumption of guilt.'

'Can you do anything then, against that evidence?'

'We can try.'

'I shouldn't be troubling you with my anxieties, I know. They aren't important, Ellen's safety is.'

Antony thought, I wish I hadn't spoken so bluntly, but surely he must have known. Aloud he said, 'You can help us, doctor, if you will.'

'Anything. Anything, of course. But I don't see—'

'Miss Gray has been a member of your household since she was eight years old.'

'She has. It was a most tragic business.'

'Will you tell me about it from your point of view.'

Clive was silent a moment. 'I think you are considering the possibility of the lesser plea that Martin mentioned,' he said at last.

'It can't be overlooked, but unless I hear something that may persuade Miss Gray to change her mind—'

'Yes, of course. But what can I tell you?'

'From your point of view.' Maitland spoke more patiently than he felt. As always, he disliked the necessity of explaining himself.

'I had always thought Edward and Madeleine an ideal couple. Certainly she appeared frantic when he was reported missing. But she pulled herself together quickly, for the sake of Ellen, she said.'

'Do you think this—' – he was fumbling for his notes, but it was noticeable that he didn't consult them – 'this

40

Michael Foster had anything to do with that?'

'In view of what happened, I find that hard to answer. It is difficult to see what motive Edward could have had except some proof of a liaison between them.'

'But that is being wise after the event.'

'In a way, I think that is true.'

'Tell me about Edward Gray. What sort of a man was he?'

'That again is difficult. We were much of an age, and saw a good deal of each other until he was abroad with the army. I always admired him. He was the sort of man people turn to in trouble, if he had gone in for medicine I think he would have had a better bedside manner than I have; but as it turned out he wasn't quite so good at dealing with his own affairs.'

'Was he level-headed?'

'He had a hair-trigger temper. That was what finally convinced me.'

'What do you think happened?'

'You know that he came back unexpectedly?'

'So I have heard.'

'It had seemed such extraordinarily bad luck, that he should be missing so soon before hostilities ceased. Well, I think he came in and found them together, nothing incriminating in that. But Madeleine would be surprised to see him, and might easily have blurted out that she wanted a divorce, something like that.'

'It could have happened that way.' Maitland half turned to Geoffrey as he spoke. 'He was extraordinarily unlucky in his judge and jury, wasn't he? Men in similar circumstances were getting off altogether at that time, I seem to remember. Or at worst with two or three years for manslaughter.'

'There were two things against him.' Horton, as usual, had an explanation ready. 'He absolutely refused to plead Guilty; that was one thing. Then there was the gun,

41

which he insisted he had left at home where anyone could have got at it. If that was true he had to go to the bureau, find it, load it. That seemed a bit cold-blooded, I expect.'

'But there was evidence ... that was one of the points of John Wilcox's evidence, wasn't it? That Gray had said he was going to take that particular gun with him on his last leave.'

'I think – don't expect logic from a jury, Antony – that in a way they believed both those things. You must remember that they thought he was lying when he pleaded Not Guilty. There was also the fact that the gun had been wiped clean of fingerprints. More cold-bloodedness.'

'I see. At least, doctor, you yourself had no doubts that your version of the affair was the correct one.'

'None at all, I'm sorry to say.'

'And the next morning, when you heard what had happened, you fetched Miss Gray.'

'Yes. The police had carried Ellen through to a neighbour's flat, and she had slept there. Edward must have been in a bewildered state of mind – not unexpectedly, I suppose – not to have had the police send for me earlier.'

'So you collected Ellen. What was her state of mind?'

'She was bewildered, too. But she didn't seem to remember anything about the night before, only waking up in a strange room.'

'What did you tell her?'

'That her mother was dead. There seemed to be no help for it. But I didn't mention her father at all. I wanted her to assume he was still away with the army.'

'How did she take the news?'

'How do you expect? There were tears at once, and outbursts of crying for a good many days afterwards. Nothing out of the ordinary.'

'And when she learned what had really happened?'

'That was different. It was nearly a year later. She'd

42

heard something from the servants, and asked me about it point blank. I told her the truth, as gently as I could. There didn't seem to be anything else to do.'

'And how did she react to that?'

'Quietly. Not a tear that I saw, but it seemed to – to weigh on her spirits. The trouble is – this isn't what you want to hear, Mr Maitland, but I must be honest with you – the trouble is, she idolised her father.'

'Yes, I must admit ... but that leads us naturally, doesn't it, to what you told her the day John Wilcox died?'

'I was aware there were questions coming. Alison had told me that Ellen had decided suddenly that her father was innocent. That seemed strange after so many years. Even when Edward died – and that was another piece of bad luck, Mr Maitland, if you're interested; it had just reached the time when we could hope for his release – even when he died, though Ellen was upset, of course, she still seemed quite willing to accept the jury's verdict.'

'I noticed that she never spoke of Edward Gray except as "my father".'

'There was a certain alienation, I think. She felt let down, as though what he did had been done to her personally. But when she began to doubt his guilt that made her all the more eager to take his part. She felt she had misjudged him. All the same, I can understand that she couldn't immediately revert to a term of affection such as "Daddy", which is what she called him before her mother's death.'

'You're giving me the impression of a rather complicated state of mind.'

William Clive sighed. 'Fairly enough, I think. She was certainly more emotional than – than I think I have ever seen her.'

'Did she tell you what had changed her mind?'

43

'A poem her mother had written.'

'On the fly-leaf of Palgrave's *Golden Treasury*. I should like to see the book, if possible.'

'Alison will find it for us. I explained to Ellen that because the verse was in her mother's handwriting, which I could see for myself it was, it didn't necessarily mean that Madeleine had composed it. But she said that didn't matter. She had written it down because she was unhappy, because it expressed some of her feelings at losing her husband, and that meant she couldn't possibly have been having an affair with Michael Foster only six months later.'

'There might be something in that.'

'It's a romantic notion,' said Doctor Clive rather testily, 'which I shouldn't have thought you'd subscribe to, Mr Maitland.'

Maitland smiled. 'I've an open mind,' he protested. 'But then, I only heard of Edward Gray for the first time last week, while your views have had time to harden over the last nineteen years.'

'Perhaps so. But all this isn't going to help Ellen,' said Clive wearily.

'Her state of mind is relevant.'

'But even if Edward was innocent, which I don't for a moment believe—'

'What would you say to the theory that John Wilcox killed Mrs Gray and Michael Foster?'

'For heaven's sake, Mr Maitland, that's sheer nonsense.'

'I'm quoting Miss Gray. And she wasn't wedded to the idea, just said she'd wondered.'

'She must be mad!' He broke off then and added after an uneasy pause, 'I don't mean that, of course. But really, it's such a stupid idea.'

'And dangerous too. I'm hoping she won't insist on giving it an airing in court.'

44

'Oh, dear, that does bring it home to me. I can't imagine Ellen in the dock.'

'I won't apologise. I think you can help her most by realising fully the gravity of her situation.'

'I'm sure you're right. But really . . . John! He was the best of good fellows, and devoted to Edward and Madeleine. But if Ellen really thought that—'

'She says it didn't occur to her until she was thinking things over in prison.'

'Then it can't have influenced her actions that night. Mr Maitland, I hoped you were going to convince me of Ellen's innocence, but instead—' He broke off there, shaking his head in a rather bewildered way.

Antony did not try to reassure him. 'You were going to tell me what you said to her that night, and what was her state of mind when she left the house.'

'Was I? Well then, she asked me about the trial, about the evidence. I gave her the case for the prosecution pretty well as it had been presented; it agreed well enough with my own view of things which I gave you a moment ago. She raised several objections, and I told her about John's evidence, which I wouldn't have done if I'd known how she'd take it. She said, "Then it was all *his* fault". And then, "I'm going to have it out with him". And she went out of the room, and I heard her running upstairs, to fetch her coat, I suppose. And then after a moment she was down again, and the front door banged behind her. I'd have remonstrated if she'd given me time, but it all happened so quickly.'

'The police,' said Horton, 'have their own theory about the gun.'

'Yes, they . . . I was questioned about that. They seemed to think that somewhere upstairs—'

'But they decided against calling you to give evidence.'

'I couldn't help them, you see.'

'Has there ever been a gun in this house?'

45

'Never. I wasn't in the Forces myself, having a slight tendency to diabetes which was discovered soon after I qualified, so there was no question of bringing home a souvenir.'

Maitland came back into the conversation. 'When Miss Gray took up target shooting—'

'So far as I know she used a gun at the club she joined.' Perhaps, if you were to be critical, there was a little too much emphasis on that statement, but Antony succeeded in catching the doctor's eye, and got a straight look in exchange for his quizzical one.

'That seems to be all for the moment,' he said then. 'Except that we'd like a word with Mrs Clive, if we may.'

'I'll call her.' The doctor heaved himself up out of his chair. 'You will remember, won't you,' – he looked from one of them to the other – 'that she has been very upset by what has happened, isn't really herself at all.' He went out into the hall, and they heard him call, 'Alison, Alison,' and then his voice rumbling on as apparently the object of his search came out of one of the other rooms.

Presently William Clive came back alone. 'My wife is just fetching the book you wanted to see,' he explained. And then, 'She's very nervous. You won't regard it, I hope.'

Both of them murmured something sympathetic, and then there was a full minute of silence before Alison Clive came into the room. Antony, coming to his feet, took the chance to study her as she crossed towards the fireplace: a woman in about as complete a contrast to her husband as well might be. For one thing, she was very thin, he thought perhaps there must be some illness there, to account for the doctor's solicitude; for another, her dark hair was very sleek and neat. Not bad-looking, if she had been less haggard, and he liked her smile as

46

she greeted them each in turn and then came closer and handed him a small, shabby, green-bound book. Palgrave's *Golden Treasury of Songs and Lyrics.*

'That's what you want, Mr Maitland,' she said. 'I don't see how it will help you.'

Inside the leaves were turning brown, but the pencilled lines were clear enough. 'Have you looked at this?' he asked. 'Do you agree with Doctor Clive that this is Mrs Gray's writing?'

'Oh, yes, there's no doubt about that.' She took the chair her husband had occupied before, and he moved to a smaller, armless one. 'Ellen seemed to think her mother had written the lines herself, and I suppose that is most likely. It's not exactly great verse, is it?'

Antony looked down at the book in his hands. As Ellen had said, it was no more than a fragment, scribbled down.

> But I only know that my heart is sore,
> And my eyes are blind with tears,
> As I turn from the path I may not tread
> And face the lonely years.

No question that Mrs Clive was right, it wasn't great verse, but something about it touched him more than he would have liked to say, something that made him think of the long-ago days when Jenny had thought him dead.

He handed the book in silence to Geoffrey, and turned to look at Alison Clive again. There seemed to be a tic under her right eye, that twitched her cheek occasionally, and her hands were clenched together in her lap; otherwise there wasn't much sign of the nervousness her husband had spoken of. 'I'm sorry to have to trouble you at such a time,' he said.

'That doesn't matter. Nothing matters but Ellen.'

'There is one thing less to worry about, my dear,' said

47

the doctor gently. 'She has assured Mr Maitland and Mr Horton that she is innocent.'

'I always said ... you know I always said, Will, that she couldn't have done it.' Her hands were pressed over her heart now, as though she felt some pain there. 'You will do your best for her, both of you, won't you?' she said.

'Certainly we shall. But I won't hide it from you, Mrs Clive, any more than I have done from your husband, that there are difficulties ahead.'

'Then what can I do for you?'

'Tell me whether, to your knowledge, there was ever a pistol in this house, of the kind—'

Before he could finish she said eagerly, 'No gun, no weapon of any kind whatever.'

'You think you can be sure of that?'

'Oh, yes, indeed.'

'You would not be familiar, for instance, with the contents of Miss Gray's chest-of-drawers?'

'You're saying Ellen had a gun hidden away.' Suddenly her voice was shrill.

The doctor murmured, 'My dear!' and made a movement as though he would have got up and gone to her side, but then apparently changed his mind and sank back in his chair again. Maitland said quietly,

'I'm saying nothing of the kind. I'm just trying to forestall the kind of questions the prosecution will ask you in court.'

'But I couldn't ... oh, no, Mr Maitland, you mustn't ask me to do that.'

'My dear,' said Doctor Clive again, 'if it will help Ellen I think you must make up your mind to it.'

'No! No, really! I couldn't.'

'Is it really necessary?' asked Clive helplessly. 'I can give evidence on that point myself.'

'In this instance, I think Mrs Clive's word would count

48

for more. Particularly if she had ever had occasion to tidy Miss Gray's things.'

'Well, I haven't. Ellen always kept her room tidy herself, and I certainly wouldn't pry.' She was calmer now, but her voice was still a little high-pitched.

'I see. In that case, Mrs Clive, we won't trouble you. But will you tell me, did you see Miss Gray on the evening of the murder?'

'Of course I did. I was here when she was asking Will about her father's trial, and I thought it wasn't wise to reopen the subject, it was all done with long ago.'

'Do you think she was right in the conclusion she had reached, that her father was not guilty?'

'No, I think it was quite unreasonable of her.'

'What was her reaction to what your husband told her?'

'She became very excited, and rushed away, and out of the house a moment later.'

'If she had a gun, it must have been somewhere handy then?'

'Yes, but I'd be no good in court.' Her hands were writhing together. 'Really, I couldn't face that.'

'Don't upset yourself, Mrs Clive. I've said we won't call you.'

'But from what you say you need my evidence,' said the doctor heavily.

'I'm afraid we do. And I'm also afraid it will give the prosecution a chance to cross-examine you about Miss Gray's demeanour that evening. I can't understand, Geoffrey,' he added in an aside to Horton, 'why they aren't calling Doctor Clive themselves.'

'One of Halloran's typical subtleties,' said Geoffrey without hesitation.

'You mean, he's counting on our calling him?'

'I certainly think he would prefer to deal with his

evidence on cross rather than on direct examination.'

'I suppose you're right,' said Maitland gloomily. 'We needn't keep you any longer, Mrs Clive, if you have things you want to do.' He noticed as he spoke that from being rather flushed she had now turned very pale, and wondered again what ailed her. 'But I'm afraid we shall have to go into things a bit more deeply with your husband.'

'Go and lie down, my dear,' Doctor Clive urged. 'A rest before lunch will do you good.' He went with her to the door – oddly enough she made no farewell to either of the visitors – and then came back to his chair again. 'I'm at your service,' he said, looking from one of them to the other. And then, 'You must excuse my wife, all this has been very hard on her.'

IV

They went back to Kempenfeldt Square for lunch, and Jenny had it waiting for them. As usual, she listened with interest to what they had to say about the case, but made no attempt to join in the conversation.

'You know everything, Geoffrey,' said Antony, taking his coffee cup to a chair by the fire. 'What's wrong with Mrs Clive?'

'You're as wise as I am. I could have told you, of course, that it was hopeless relying on her evidence. She made that very clear when I saw them earlier.'

'Do you think ... I thought she was concerned for her niece in spite of that.'

'Oh, yes, I think her refusal is genuine enough. She knows she'd go to pieces under cross-examination.'

'Well, we must make the best of what we have. Not Ellen, unless she changes her mind again ... and I wouldn't put it past her. Doctor Clive, and I wish there was any way out of that, because once Halloran gets his claws into him—'

'We've got to have some sort of confirmation that Ellen didn't own a gun. Besides, the jury will already be suspicious because she isn't giving evidence, if we didn't call her guardian either that would just about put paid to all our chances.'

'Which are slim at best. Then there's the housekeeper and charlady, both of whom had something to do with cleaning her room. After that only Stephen Langland, and character evidence from two old friends of her parents, Martin Roydon and Frederick Tate. The prosecution's case leaves us with precious little room for manoeuvre, but you know that.'

'Do you want to see any of these people?'

'Time enough in court. It was Ellen's background I was curious about, but I'm afraid my curiosity hasn't helped matters at all.'

'I could have told you—'

'Yes, Geoffrey, but that isn't helpful either.'

'I suppose not. You do realise the case may come on at any time, don't you?'

'Don't worry. I'll give the brief priority.'

Horton drank the rest of his coffee rather quickly. 'I must be getting back to the office,' he said. 'Do you want a lift?'

'No, I need a walk. Anyway, I'd like another cup of coffee.'

It was Jenny who saw the visitor out. She came back to the living-room to find that her husband had abandoned his chair and taken up his favourite position with his back to the fire. She plumped up a cushion absent-mindedly, and said, not looking at him, 'You're worried about something, Antony.'

'Not really, it's just ... not my favourite kind of case,

love. A girl I like, and whom I'm sorry for, and who's as guilty as hell.'

'You've defended guilty people before. In fact, you say that by far the majority of cases—'

'So I have,' he said, not comforted. 'This girl is stubborn, and the line she insists on following will earn her an unnecessarily hard sentence, I'm afraid.'

'If she killed this man—'

'There are extenuating circumstances, at least I think there are. What do you think it would do to a child to know that her father was in prison for murdering her mother, and her mother's lover as well? And then, when she suddenly persuaded herself he was innocent after all, wouldn't she be ready to fly off the handle in his defence?'

'Is that what you think happened?'

'She won't admit it, but it's perfectly obvious.'

'And if she persists in pleading Not Guilty—?'

'They'll throw the book at her,' said Antony inelegantly. He turned to put down his empty cup on the mantelpiece. 'I should be getting along too, if there's to be anything left of the afternoon. Besides, Mallory is annoyed with me for disturbing his carefully planned schedules, so a show of diligence may not come amiss.'

'You really shouldn't let Mr Mallory bully you,' said Jenny, following him to the door.

Antony grinned at her. 'Show me how to stop him,' he said.

PART TWO

REGINA VERSUS GRAY

1965

WEDNESDAY, the first day of the trial

I

Bruce Halloran Q.C. was a friend of Sir Nicholas Harding's and thought he knew Antony Maitland very well indeed. In fact he was even, in his own way, fond of him (which would have surprised Antony), without approving of him in the slightest degree. He was a swarthy man, tall and rather heavily built, and with a booming voice that could raise the echoes if he didn't remember to moderate it in some degree. He came into the courtroom that Wednesday morning with a supremely confident air (and why shouldn't he feel confident? thought Maitland a little sourly), greeted his opponent and his junior, Derek Stringer, and went on to take his place beside his own junior, a youngish man called Palmer, who was said – on what grounds nobody knew – to have a bright future ahead of him. Then Halloran leaned across to say to Maitland, in a whisper that was clearly audible in every corner of the room, 'Pity O'Brien was taken ill. No rabbits out of the hat today, my lad.' He was completely oblivious of the fact that anyone could hear this highly improper comment besides the man to whom it was addressed.

Maitland contented himself with looking enigmatic, which wouldn't deceive Halloran for a minute, of course. Halloran smiled, and became apparently absorbed in his brief.

They weren't kept waiting long. Mr Justice Carruthers was noted for his punctuality, as he was also known with some gratitude by counsel for not sitting overlong. You could count on an hour with your brief before dinner, if you felt so inclined; or on a leisurely drink, if that was more to your taste. He was as aware as Counsel for the Prosecution that the defence brief hadn't been offered to Maitland in the first place, and thought it would be interesting to see him fighting a battle where the guilt of the defendant was not in question. At least, that must be assumed from the original choice of counsel; Kevin O'Brien was a great one for lost causes.

Meanwhile, there was the prisoner to consider. A nice-looking young woman, the judge thought, but so pale that he was relieved when the first formalities were over and he could see her seated in the dock. No indication so far that the defence meant to go for 'diminished responsibility', though considering her background he would be inclined to give them a good deal of latitude. But Horton was a good man; she would have been well advised.

And now Halloran was well into his opening address. '... but in the circumstances I shall ask your patience while I inform you briefly of some of the background to this case. The prisoner, while no more than eight years old, underwent what I am sure you will consider a traumatic experience—' And here was Maitland, on his feet with an objection, when his opponent was plainly in a conciliatory mood. Mr Justice Carruthers looked for a long moment at Counsel for the Defence, who met his look steadily enough, but wished himself anywhere at all except in Number One Court at the Old Bailey. It seemed an age before the judge spoke.

'I think we must allow Mr Halloran to elaborate his theme a little, Mr Maitland. I will intervene myself if I feel he is taking too much licence.'

'I am obliged to your lordship.' He sat down with a feeling that for a moment was almost anger: the old boy thinks *I* advised her to fight the case on a straight Not Guilty plea. But I should have foreseen that, shouldn't I? I bet Geoffrey did. He turned his head for a moment to look at his instructing solicitor, but Horton's face told him nothing.

Meanwhile, Halloran was going on with his recital, his big voice, which could have filled a much larger space than the courtroom, muted out of consideration for his listeners ... especially, of course, the jury. He was a formidable opponent (well, Antony knew that already), the more so because he never exaggerated, never tried to make a fact do more work than it was able. Juries respected his moderation, and when he did occasionally leap to the attack felt that he must be well justified. So the story of Edward Gray unfolded in the courtroom, and Maitland looked to be half asleep (but that wouldn't deceive anyone, least of all Halloran) while he waited for the point he knew must be coming where he must intervene again. Heaven send Carruthers was in a patient mood!

'... and I need not elaborate for you the effect this must have had on a small, highly-strung girl. It seems that all through the years she thought her father guilty, but that something happened on the tenth of November last – members of the jury, I must ask you to remember that date – something happened, I say, that made her for the first time—'

'My lord, I must protest!'

The judge turned on him his rather mournful regard. He was a small man, whom Maitland, with no great originality, had been known to liken to an intelligent bloodhound. 'What is troubling you, Mr Maitland?' he enquired.

'My lord, as I understand it, my learned friend has no basis in the evidence for these allegations.'

'Well, Mr Halloran?'

57

'The prisoner's own statement, m'lud—'

'Should not be admitted,' said Maitland firmly, for all the world as if he were sure of his ground. 'It was made in the absence of her solicitor, when she was in a state of shock.'

'Shock?' said Halloran in a pleased tone, choosing to forget for a moment that he should be addressing the bench.

'My lord, you can imagine the effect on a young woman who had just discovered, inadvertently, the body of a dear friend.'

To Antony's exasperation, Halloran could be quite clearly heard to murmur to himself, 'Inadvertently,' with a questioning lilt, as though he were trying to appreciate the aptness of the word. The judge leaned forward. 'Mr Maitland, if this statement was taken in due form by the police, after the proper warning had been given—'

'I am not disputing that, my lord.'

'Then I think I must overrule your objection. You may proceed, Mr Halloran.'

And proceed he did. The poem, the questions to Doctor Clive, the angry reaction, the lot. And then there were the events of the evening of November the eleventh. A damning recital. It was amusing to think (only he seemed to have lost his capacity for amusement, just at the moment) that if Ellen had taken his and Geoffrey's advice Halloran would be doing half their job for them. And here was Carruthers thinking, most likely, that he was fighting the case straight, with no plea of mitigating circumstances, from some cock-eyed idea of enhancing his own reputation. Well, there was no help for that. But he didn't like it, he didn't like it one little bit, only what could you do with a stubborn client? She had a right to be represented.

Then came the witnesses. The policeman who had

been first on the scene, let Derek deal with him. 'You say that there seemed to be some sort of angry feeling between the accused and the two children of the deceased. But that is only an idea, is it not? You couldn't produce any evidence, any proof?' The ballistics expert, the fingerprint expert, the medical evidence, all quite straightforward, nothing for the defence there; nor in the brief evidence of the man who produced a scale plan of the Wilcoxes' flat. Barbara Wilcox ... now that was a different matter.

She was a tall girl, and slim, with fair, straight hair that fell to her shoulders and – unusual combination – rather beautiful brown eyes. She was nervous, which wasn't to be wondered at, but she was making a good impression. A nice girl in difficult circumstances. Halloran was being gentle with her, his booming voice quieted still further. Her name, her address, her age; she had been seventeen last week, and was still a schoolgirl.

'This must be very distressing for you, Miss Wilcox. I will try not to keep you longer than I can help.'

'It's all right. I told them – the police – and the other man who came to see us that I wanted to give evidence.'

'That will make my task the easier. Will you tell us what happened on the evening of the eleventh of November last?'

'Yes, I – we were playing table-tennis, my brother and I, in the dining-room of our home.' An interval while the plan was produced. 'Yes, that is correct, the room on the right of the main entrance. We were playing, and there was the sound of a car backfiring, at least that was what I thought it was, and then I realised it had sounded louder than it could have done from our flat, which is upstairs, you know. So I said to Roy, "We'd better see what's up".'

'And he came with you, Miss Wilcox?'

'Yes, of course. We went out into the hall, and the

59

drawing-room door was standing open, which was un-usual when there was anybody there. And, of course, we both knew Dad was at home. So I went straight across there and through the open door, and just got a glimpse of Dad lying back in his chair, with Ellen standing look-ing down at him, and then she whirled round and prac-tically pushed us out of the room.'

'I am sorry to interrupt you, Miss Wilcox, but I should like you to tell us again exactly what you saw through the open door.'

'Why ... my father was dead, but I didn't know it then. He was lying back in his chair—'

'As if he was asleep?'

'Not at all like that. With his head thrown right back. I didn't think of it then, but he'd have been uncom-fortable like that, if he'd been alive.'

'And what else did you see?'

'Ellen Gray standing looking at him with the gun in her hand, and then she dropped it and came across the room to us and said, "Don't come in here. Your father needs a doctor." So I went out with her into the hall, but Roy stayed behind.'

'And after that?'

'He came out looking very pale and – and grim, and said—'

'He will tell us what he said, Miss Wilcox. What did he do then?'

'He telephoned for the police.'

'What was Miss Gray doing all this time?'

'She was just standing. I suppose she was shocked by what she had done.'

'My lord—'

'Yes, Mr Halloran, that won't do you know,' said the judge, looking up.

'Certainly not, m'lud,' agreed Halloran cheerfully. The jury had certainly noticed what the witness had said. 'If you could just tell us, Miss Wilcox, without drawing any conclusions, how the prisoner looked, what she said.'

'She looked stunned. She just said, "Barbara dear, I'm so sorry", and something the same when Roy came out to telephone. Then we ... just waited. It was horrible, but what else could we do? I didn't feel I wanted to talk to Ellen ... ever again.'

There was some reiteration, of course, but that was the gist of her evidence. Carruthers adjourned for the luncheon recess before the cross-examination, which left Maitland in a jittery mood. The girl seemed calm enough, you might almost say a little cold, but if he succeeded in upsetting her that wouldn't be popular with the jury. And yet ...

After the recess he plunged straight into the middle of things. 'How long a time would you say elapsed between your hearing the shot and going to investigate?'

'I thought ... five minutes.' Already her replies sounded more tentative. 'You see, I didn't think at first—'

'No, we understand that, Miss Wilcox. The last thing you would have expected to hear. What was Miss Gray doing when you went into the drawing-room?'

'I told—'

He smiled at her. 'Tell me again.'

'She was standing looking down at my father with the gun in her hand.'

'Then – you said – she dropped it and came across the room to try to dissuade you from entering.'

'That's right.'

'We are not disputing that Miss Gray picked up the gun when she came into the room.' That was meant for the jury, but he was still addressing the witness with what Derek Stringer, taking the note beside him, mentally categorised as gentle reasonableness. He knew his leader in this mood. 'But that was only a moment before you did,' Maitland went on.

'So she says.'

He made no protest at that, though it was certain he noticed the comment, being totally absorbed by now in what he was doing. 'Don't you think it is a more reasonable explanation than that she shot your father, and then stood over him for five full minutes with the gun in her hand?' he said, and sat down before she had time to formulate an answer. Barbara was left looking a little uncertainly about her, but Halloran declined to re-examine, and a moment later her place was taken by her brother.

Roy Wilcox had come into court in a belligerent mood. At fourteen years old – nearly fifteen – that wasn't to be wondered at. He was almost as tall as his sister, and very like her without being in the least womanish in appearance. He answered Halloran's questions with commendable conciseness, which couldn't fail, Maitland thought, to make an impression. But if the jury believed what he was telling them, that only a few seconds had passed between their hearing the shot and going to investigate, then it was all up with Ellen Gray, and nothing he could say or do would make any difference.

The examination-in-chief passed without incident, exactly according to proof. But when Roy turned slightly to face Counsel for the Defence there was the unmistakable light of battle in his eye. Maitland could sympathise with him, but it was going to be tricky. Very tricky indeed.

He started out cautiously, something surely unexceptionable. 'You told my friend that there was nothing special about the evening your father died, nothing to single it out from any other evening until the tragedy occurred.'

'Yes.'

62

'Your mother was out, your father was in the drawing-room, reading. You and your sister in the dining-room, playing table tennis.'

'That's right. Look here, I already—'

'You must forgive me. I wanted to have everything clear in my own mind. And yet, in spite of this normalcy, you jumped immediately to the conclusion that the noise you heard was the sound of a shot, not a car backfiring in the street outside.'

'I didn't think anything about it. It was Barbara.'

'But you went with her to investigate?'

'Yes, I did.'

'In a few seconds, you say. A few seconds after hearing this unidentifiable sound.'

'That's right.'

'Let us be a little more accurate. How many seconds, exactly?'

'I couldn't tell you.'

'Five, perhaps? Ten?'

'Something like that.'

'Something like ten seconds?'

'I don't really know,' said Roy unhappily. 'Only it wasn't long.'

'I see. Not so long as five minutes, for instance?'

'Not nearly so long.'

'Are you sure about that?'

'Quite sure,' said the witness, recovering his truculence.

'How much shorter a time?'

'I don't know.'

'You said, "it wasn't long", didn't you? Five minutes isn't very long, is it?'

'No, but—'

'What you are really saying is that you have very little idea.'

'It wasn't long,' said Roy stubbornly.

'Then we will leave it there. You followed your sister into the drawing-room, and there saw ... what?'

'You haven't a very good memory, have you?' ('*Mr Halloran,*' said the judge.)

'I know. You told my learned friend. But let's pretend that I wasn't here, or wasn't paying attention just then.'

'Oh, very well! Dad was dead—'

'Was that immediately apparent to you?'

'No, of course not. He was just lying back in his chair in rather an awkward position. And Ellen was standing looking at him, and then she turned and tried to shoo us out of the room. Barbara went, but I stayed to look at Dad, and then I saw he was dead, and there was blood—'

'Never mind that. Where was the gun?'

'In the chair where Ellen dropped it.'

'Did you see her do that?'

'No.'

'Was she holding the gun when you went into the room?'

'No.' He went on quickly as Maitland opened his mouth to speak again. 'At least, I don't think so.'

'Your sister says—'

'Yes, I know. I won't argue, she may be right.'

'I see. And after that?'

'I went out into the hall, where Barbara and Ellen were.'

'What were they doing?'

'Nothing. At least, I didn't notice, I was fairly upset. I know Ellen said something about being sorry, which seemed pretty good cheek in the circumstances. And I went to telephone the police. They came rather quickly.'

'Thank you. Just to refresh my memory on one point, and then I won't bother you any further. You aren't at

64

all sure, are you, how long it was between your hearing the shot and going to investigate?'

'It wasn't long.'

'That is such a vague phrase. You're not really sure, are you?'

'Not exactly,' said the witness, floundering. Halloran came to his feet.

'If your lordship pleases, my friend is labouring his point.'

'Because it is an important one,' said Maitland, not waiting for the judge to speak.

'All the same, Mr Maitland, I think—'

'As your lordship pleases. I have no further questions,' said Maitland, sitting down with a martyred air. But Halloran thought it important enough to go through the question of what happened on the evening of November the eleventh all over again.

The next witness was the secretary of the Hand-gun Club which Ellen Gray had attended. His name was Horace Dinsdale, and he was clearly uncomfortable at finding himself in the spotlight. The reason soon emerged.

Miss Gray, it seemed, had come as the guest of a member, Stephen Langland, but had not been by any means regular in her attendance. Last summer, for instance, they had hardly seen her. He couldn't say how her performance was, he had never heard of her shooting in competition with any other member.

'To turn from that matter for the moment,' said Halloran, and his tone would have alerted Maitland even if he had not already known what was coming, 'we come to what happened on the sixth of November last. One of your members approached you—'

'Mr Forbes. He said he had a Mauser automatic pistol, for which he had never had a licence. It was a war souvenir. He'd thought of handing it in during one

of the amnesties, but that seemed a waste, so he suggested that I should take it over for the club. Of course,
it was a bit irregular, but I could get a licence quite
easily, so I locked it away in my desk drawer until I could
apply for one. But when I came to look for it again it
was gone. The lock was quite a simple one, I have opened
it myself with a paper knife before now, when I mislaid
the key.'

'So that anybody that knew that the pistol was there—'

'It certainly wasn't a secret from the members. I mentioned it myself to several of them.'

There was an interval there, while one of the exhibits
was shown to the witness. 'Is that the same gun?' Halloran asked.

'It's the same make, the same calibre, similar in
every way. But I couldn't positively identify it. I never
had occasion to take a note of the serial number, you
know.'

'When did you notice that the pistol was missing?'

'On the ninth. That was the Monday.'

'And had Miss Gray visited the club in the intervening
period?'

'My records show that she was there on the seventh.'

'Thank you, Mr Dinsdale, that will be all.' He
glanced from the witness, who was preparing to leave the
box, to his learned friend, Mr Maitland, who was coming
to his feet. 'I seem to have misled you, Mr Dinsdale. The
defence has still some questions for you.'

The witness didn't actually say, 'Oh, my ears and
whiskers!' but it was, Maitland felt, touch and go for a
moment. The poor little man looked scared to death.
He felt a moment's amused sympathy with Halloran;
not a good crutch to take almost the full weight of your
argument. If he could be befuddled . . .

'A few very simple questions,' said Maitland soothingly, 'which should not detain you long. You remember,

66

of course, the day Mr Forbes gave you the Mauser automatic we are discussing.'

'Yes, of course I do.'

'Did you have much conversation about the gun?'

'Very little.'

'Did he say, for instance, "This is a Mauser automatic pistol"?'

'No, nothing like that. He just said he had a hand-gun that might interest me, and when I assented he handed it over.'

'And then, of course, you examined it?'

'Not really. It was so very irregular, you know. I put it straight into the drawer.'

'And locked the drawer?'

'Yes.'

'You say you discovered the gun was missing on the ninth. How many times had you looked at it in the intervening period?'

'I hadn't looked at it at all.'

'But from the brief glance you had of it you can tell us its make quite certainly.'

'Oh, yes.'

'On what do you base your certainty? On sight? But you saw it, on your own admission, for a moment only. On the feel of it in your hand? But any gun of similar design and weight—'

'It was a Mauser automatic,' said the witness stubbornly.

'So you say. But you must give us your evidence for that "fact", Mr Dinsdale.'

'I am familiar with all sorts of hand-guns.'

'I am not denying your expertise. But in this case—'

'I identified it by sight, I suppose, as much as anything else.'

'After no more than a moment.' The witness was

silent. 'Come, Mr Dinsdale, will you not admit even the possibility that you were wrong?'

('M'lud,' said Halloran; and, 'No, Mr Halloran,' said the judge, almost in the same breath.)

'I—' said the witness hesitantly, 'I think—'

'But that isn't enough for us, Mr Dinsdale. You must be sure.'

'I was sure. I never thought about it till I came here, that it might have been something else.'

'The same make but a different calibre, for instance? Or the same calibre, but a different make?'

'I ... don't ... know.'

'Thank you, Mr Dinsdale. Then you cannot say, can you, that it was similar in any way to the gun you were shown today?'

'It was like, very like,' said the witness, with one last flash of spirit. But Maitland had already seated himself. Halloran re-examined briefly, but this only seemed to demoralise Mr Dinsdale still further.

'Not unsatisfactory,' said Horton for counsel's ear only, and Maitland grinned at him.

The next witness was the aforementioned Mr Forbes, who rejoiced – or most probably didn't – in the Christian name of Algernon. He might have been made to specification from the defence's blueprint. The gun had been given to him, or rather left in his care, by his brother, who had since died. No, he himself couldn't tell you its make, didn't know one gun from another except for the target pistol he used at the club. The exhibit shown to him might have been the same one, or it might not. He hadn't been through the war himself, never had anything to do with guns; a conscientious objector, worked on a farm for the duration.

'But surely, Mr Forbes,' said Halloran a little testily at this point, 'your membership of the Hand-gun Club—'

'I have a good eye,' the witness told him, not without

some self-satisfaction, 'and target shooting doesn't do anybody any harm.'

All Derek Stringer had to do, when Halloran had finished with this unsatisfactory material, was to see that one or two points were stressed, in case the jury had missed them the first time around.

After that there came the police officer, now retired, who had been responsible for the investigation into the murder of Madeleine Gray and Michael Foster, and the chief witness at Edward Gray's trial. His confirmation was merely required that John Wilcox's evidence had been part of the prosecution's case; and again this would have been helpful to the defence if they had been fighting as both Maitland and Horton had wished on the grounds of 'diminished responsibility'. As it was, Maitland objected again as to the admissibility of the evidence, and was again overruled. So all that could be done was to gain from the witness an admission, freely given, that Wilcox's evidence had only been part of a well-rounded case, that no reasonable person could have regarded him as the sole villain in the condemnation of Edward Gray. And even that might not meet with their client's unqualified approval, the ensuing argument could be made to cut both ways.

And then came the adjournment, a little later than was customary with Mr Justice Carruthers. 'Perhaps he got interested,' said Maitland cynically to his junior as they left the court. And then, 'A pleasant day tomorrow, starting with Inspector Conway's evidence, first thing. Tell you what, I'll toss you for him.' But they both knew that cross-examining Detective-Inspector Conway was an honour that the leading counsel for the defence couldn't decline.

II

He aired his grievance again that evening to an audience consisting of Jenny, curled up in her favourite corner of the sofa with a coffee cup balanced dangerously on the arm, and their friend, Roger Farrell, who had dropped in after leaving his wife, Meg (better known to the public as Margaret Hamilton) at the theatre. 'I always get off on the wrong foot with Conway,' he said gloomily. 'Somehow it seems unavoidable, he just doesn't like me.'

'Have you ever done anything to make him like you?' Jenny asked, concerned, as always, to be fair.

'No, I haven't. I don't go about trying to curry favour with the police,' Antony protested. Roger laughed.

'I've heard you on the subject of Inspector Conway before,' he said. 'It happens sometimes ... a sort of mutual antipathy.'

'That's all very well, but I *don't* dislike him. It's only that he's so damned disapproving about everything that the temptation to say something to annoy him just seems irresistible sometimes.'

'There, you see, it's all your own fault,' said Jenny. Both the men looked at her in surprise at this uncharacteristic announcement, but when she went on Antony, at least, understood. 'Anyway, it can't matter tomorrow. The worst that can happen will be a headline in the papers, "Defence counsel clashes with police witness," which can't do any harm at all.'

'It might harm my client.'

'No, because he's a witness for the prosecution. You're supposed to harass him,' said Jenny triumphantly. It was clear that for all she cared her husband might be on bad terms with every policeman in the kingdom, so long as there was nothing personal about it.

70

Antony was amused by this version of his professional duties, and said so. 'You mustn't encourage me in bad habits, love,' he added. 'A witness should not be antagonised unless it's absolutely necessary, particularly when you're trying to disprove his story.'

'Well, I can't see that it matters at all,' said Jenny, unrepentant.

Roger was smiling too. 'All that aside,' he said, when he saw that Antony did not seem disposed to carry the argument further, 'how do you think the case is going?'

'It can't go any way but badly.' Antony was gloomy again. 'They've got a case and we haven't, it's as simple as that. And trust Halloran to make the most of it. But that wouldn't be so bad if Carruthers didn't think I'm playing dice with my client's freedom for some purpose of my own. I like Carruthers,' he complained.

'I don't quite follow that, I'm afraid,' said Roger doubtfully.

'Carruthers is the judge—'

'Yes, I know that from the papers.'

'—and what he thinks I should be doing is admitting Ellen's guilt and claiming that she wasn't altogether responsible for her actions. Because of the background of her unhappy childhood, that would really go down well with the jury; her ambivalent feelings for her father; and her sudden conviction – however unreasonable, in fact the more unreasonable the better – her sudden conviction that an injustice had been done him.'

'I think I see.'

'I'm sure you do. It's what I advised her to do, and Geoffrey had already had a go at her on the same lines, of course. But there was no doing anything with her. Hence these tears.'

'What difference will it make to your client?'

'The difference between a life sentence and the two or

three years which, if we'd softened up Carruthers properly, is probably what he'd have given her.'

'It is quite unreasonable,' said Jenny, 'to blame yourself.'

'Quite unreasonable,' Antony was smiling again.
'What can't be cured must be endured,' he said, looking
from one of them to the other. 'And I know I started
the subject, but for heaven's sake let's talk about something else!'

THURSDAY, the second day of the trial

I

Detective-Inspector Conway was a thin-faced man with
a square jaw, a tight-lipped look, and (as Antony knew
well enough) an acid tongue. He gave his evidence, in
answer to Halloran's questions, as if he disapproved
of the whole unsavoury business. There was certainly
no bias there, but the trouble was his attitude lent, if
anything, a good deal of credibility to what he was
saying.

The police evidence was in most respects a reiteration
of what Halloran had said in his opening speech about
the murder of John Wilcox. The question of the
accused's statement came up, and Maitland protested
again as in duty bound, but without very much hope of
success. That was just as well, Mr Justice Carruthers
overruled him, and the statement was duly read into the
record. It stressed all the wrong things, of course, and in
the face of it there was no doubt that Ellen Gray had had
– or had thought she had – good reason to be angry with
the deceased. Maitland fumed inwardly, and was in a
fighting mood when at last he rose to cross-examine. Just
the sort of mood, as Sir Nicholas could have told him, to
be avoided when dealing with someone of Conway's
temper.

'You tell us, Inspector, that the gun found in the chair
in the Wilcoxes' drawing-room had been handled by my
client.'

'It had.'

'And that this same pistol was certainly the one that fired the shot that killed John Wilcox.'

'If you listened to Inspector Benton's evidence—' began Conway, poker-faced, but he was not allowed to continue.

'Yes, I heard what your ballistics expert had to say. You are not arguing with his conclusions, are you? Your contention is the same?'

'Certainly.' A moment ago it would have been difficult to see how the inspector's manner could become any stiffer, but somehow he managed it.

'And you further contend, if I understand you rightly, that it is the same pistol that was stolen from the Hand-gun Club.'

'It would explain how it came into the prisoner's possession,' said Conway incautiously, and Maitland, who was completely concentrated on the witness now – for all he knew they might have been alone in the courtroom – pounced on the statement eagerly.

'I have yet to learn that there is any need for explanation. There is no proof that it is the same pistol . . . is there, Inspector?'

'No proof, no.'

'And no proof that Ellen Gray ever had a weapon of any kind in her possession, for that matter.' He waited a moment, but the witness did not choose to comment, and he went on scathingly. 'Your logic is faulty, Inspector. The person who killed John Wilcox owned or had access to a gun, therefore Ellen Gray . . . you're twisting the facts to suit your theory, and the whole thing falls to the ground on a faulty premise.'

Conway was normally a pale man, but now two angry spots of colour had appeared, high on his cheekbones. 'I have tried to present the evidence fairly,' he said, and his voice shook a little with the effort at control. 'It seems to me that it is you who are twisting facts.'

74

'It is a fact, is it not, that there is no proof that the gun that killed John Wilcox is the same gun that was stolen from the Hand-gun Club?'

'No proof, but a strong presumption.'

'Made to fit your theory. I don't like your case, Inspector.'

'It is not "my" case, as you call it.'

'The prosecution's case, then. You provided the ammunition, didn't you?'

'Mr Maitland!' said Carruthers mildly.

'My lord?'

'The witness is here in the course of his duty. I do not feel it is right for you to attack him in this way.'

'My lord, the prosecution's case—'

'Does not rest entirely on this one point, as he has very properly reminded you.'

'As your lordship pleases,' said Maitland mutinously, the words "very properly" being in the circumstances in the nature of a red rag to a bull. 'I will ask you then, Inspector,' he added, this time with studied politeness, 'upon what day the gun is supposed to have been removed from the premises of the Hand-gun Club?'

'Our information is that the prisoner was at the club on the seventh of November.'

'But according to her statement – you are relying on her statement on this point, are you not? – she knew nothing at that point of the course of her father's trial, nothing of what you say she chose to think of as John Wilcox's perfidy—'

'She says herself in her statement that she blamed him,' said the witness hotly, interrupting counsel in full flight.

'We are not now considering Miss Gray's statement,' said Maitland, with some of the illogicality of which he had accused Conway a moment before. 'I am asking you what motive she could have had for stealing the gun on the seventh of November, when her motive for the murder – her so-called motive – did not exist until the eleventh of that month?'

'We have only the accused's word—'

'Upon which the prosecution are relying. You ought to know that, as you yourself read her statement into evidence.'

'Well, I don't think it is up to me to explain anything.'

Halloran had half risen in his seat, and succeeded in catching the judge's eye. 'Yes, Mr Halloran,' said Carruthers, a little wearily. 'The witness is perfectly correct in what he says, Mr Maitland. It is not for him to explain any anomalies in the evidence.'

'Certainly not, my lord.' Counsel sounded properly shocked. But he couldn't resist adding, 'So long as he admits they are anomalies,' which brought a frown to the judicial brow, and put Maitland irreverently in mind of a bloodhound who had forgotten where a particularly juicy bone was buried. Suppressing the thought, he turned back to the witness.

'According to this theory of yours, of the prosecution's, whichever you prefer, Miss Gray had the gun in her possession from the seventh to the eleventh of November. She was living, let me remind you, in her uncle's house. Have you been able to find anybody who saw the pistol during that period?'

'No.'

'You admit that?' He used the phrase with a rather fierce satisfaction. It had been a thing Conway had asked of him on an occasion in the past when their positions were reversed, and he himself had been under the hated necessity of answering questions. The detective reacted by managing to look even stiffer and more disapproving than ever.

'It isn't a matter of admitting—'

'Oh, but I think it is. I think a great deal of the background of this case depends on someone's preconceived notions.'

'M'lud,' said Halloran, in a voice that went booming round the courtroom. Even the judge looked faintly startled, but he wasn't slow in responding.

'I agree, Mr Halloran. Mr Maitland, I think—'

'As your lordship pleases,' said Maitland, who in any case had said all he wished to on the subject. 'You say, Inspector, that you can bring no evidence that Miss Gray had the gun concealed at her home during the four days prior to the murder.'

'That is true.'

'In spite of the fact that you yourself, and some of your energetic young men, no doubt, questioned everybody who could conceivably have had the chance to see it.'

'Our enquiries—'

'Which were thorough, Inspector, I am sure.'

'—yielded no results,' said Conway steadily, declining to be put off his stroke by counsel's sudden affability.

'I see.' Maitland sounded thoughtful now. 'There is also the question of motive. I hasten to add, my lord,' he added, turning deferentially to the judge, 'that I should not be bringing up the subject at all if my client's statement had not been admitted. But as the prosecution seem to be relying on that as explaining what is otherwise inexplicable—'

'You may proceed, Mr Maitland,' said Carruthers. Antony could almost have sworn he was amused. 'With caution,' he added in an admonitory tone. But then, catching sight of the old-fashioned pocket watch which he generally placed on the bench in front of him, he added firmly, 'After luncheon, if you please. We will take a recess until two o'clock.'

'Just when I was getting Conway going nicely,' Maitland grumbled as they left the court. Derek Stringer sym-

77

pathised, but Horton chose to read him a lecture on the pitfalls in the path of counsel who got on the wrong side of the judge. 'All very well,' said Antony, cheering up immediately at the hint of opposition, 'but I know Carruthers. He doesn't know what the hell we're up to – I'm not too sure myself, half the time – but I'm beginning to think he's willing to wait and see.'

'I wish him joy of the experience,' said Geoffrey crossly. Antony laughed and took his arm.

'If we hurry with lunch you'd have time for a word with our client before we reconvene,' he suggested. 'She's a self-possessed lass, but I thought once or twice this morning she was looking a bit lonely.'

II

So after lunch it was all to go over again, cautiously, as the judge had advised him. Horton thought perhaps his words of wisdom had done some good, and relaxed a little, pleased with himself and – for the moment – with counsel. In spite of this, Conway's temper was visibly wearing thin when Maitland reached the only new ground he was to cover. 'There is now the question of motive,' he said, as he had done before the adjournment, and was, for once in his life, alert for Carruthers's reaction. 'You have chosen to introduce my client's own statement, and are relying on this to persuade the jury that she had, in fact, a reason for what would otherwise have seemed a completely senseless crime.'

'Her own words—' Conway began, but was interrupted enthusiastically by counsel.

'Yes, precisely. That is what I should like to do. Examine her own words and see if they will really bear the interpretation the prosecution has put on them.'

'I think you will find that they are capable of only one interpretation.'

'Well, we shall see. Have you a copy of the statement there?' A moment later one was handed to the witness by the usher. 'That is better. If you will turn to the second page, Inspector—'

Conway turned over the first sheet, rather as though it had offended him personally in some way, and glared angrily at the second. 'Well?' he said, after counsel had let the silence lengthen a little.

'You mustn't be impatient with me, Inspector,' said Maitland dulcetly; anyone who knew them both would have seen the likeness to Sir Nicholas very clearly marked in that moment. 'The second paragraph from the bottom ... if you would be kind enough to read it for us.'

'On the eleventh of November I asked my uncle for the first time about my father's trial.'

Maitland interrupted him. 'That is an important point, in view of the prosecution's contention that the gun was removed from the Hand-gun Club several days before.'

The judge was leaning forward before Halloran could lumber to his feet. 'You will have plenty of opportunity of addressing the jury later, Mr Maitland.'

'I am grateful to your lordship for the reminder. If you will proceed, Inspector.'

'It was quite clear to me from what he said that John Wilcox had been one of the principal witnesses against him. That made me very angry, and I decided to have it out with him straight away.'

'Just a minute! How many times in your life has something made you "very angry", Inspector?'

Another man might have been amused by the question, Conway merely glowered. 'You're not very pleased with me at the moment, are you?' asked counsel insinuatingly.

'I have to admit—' said the detective in a shaken voice, but he wasn't allowed to continue.

'Precisely! You're hiding it well, but I could almost say you're "very angry", couldn't I? But you won't take the first opportunity to murder me, will you? At least, I hope not.'

'I hope I shall have sufficient self-control to refrain,' said Conway, with a glimmer of humour that immediately made Maitland feel more friendly towards him.

'But you would admit – wouldn't you? –' he insisted, 'that the words can be used with a great deal less than murderous intent.'

'Of course they can, but—'

'M'lud,' said Halloran.

'Yes, Mr Halloran. I think we have had enough of this line of questioning. What the witness might or might not do,' Carruthers added, turning to the jury, 'is not evidence in any sense of the word.'

'Then I have no further questions,' said Maitland, with a martyred air that amused the judge as much as it annoyed his opponent. 'There is, after all,' he added, in an audible aside to his junior, 'as his lordship reminded me, still my closing speech.'

That ended the case for the prosecution. Maitland made his opening remarks brief, but he thought he could sense the feeling in the courtroom hardening against Ellen when it was realised that she wouldn't be giving evidence, but he still didn't regret her decision. If she repeated and emphasised what had already been said in her statement – as she certainly would – it couldn't do anything but harm. But he was decidedly unhappy with his tiny array of witnesses, and rose to examine the first of them, Doctor William Clive, with distinct reluctance.

None of this showed in his manner, however, as he took the doctor through the preliminary questions. 'You have known my client, Miss Ellen Gray, all her life, I believe,' he asked, when this was done.

'Certainly. I was related to her mother, and a close friend of both her parents.'

'And after her mother's death and her father's trial you adopted her?'

'Not formally. There was no question of it, as her father was still alive. When he died she was already eighteen years old.'

'I see. But she has lived in your household since she was only eight.'

'Yes. It has been a very happy time for my wife and myself.'

'That's interesting, doctor. You couldn't say that, for instance, if she had ever shown signs of having a murderous temperament.'

Halloran turned his head and looked at Maitland, but let the moment go by. 'Of course not,' said the witness stoutly. 'She has always been a very – a very gentle girl.'

'Can you tell us something of the composition of the household. Your wife and yourself—'

'We have a housekeeper, who lives in. And a cleaning woman twice a week for the heavier work.'

'Would Miss Gray clean her own room, for instance?'

'No, there was no question of that since she went out to work every day.'

'Who would look after it then?'

'My wife might go in to tidy round, and the housekeeper to make the bed and dust, and so on. And the charwoman would go in, once or twice a week, I don't really know.'

'Your wife is in ill health, I believe. That is the sole reason she isn't here to give evidence.'

'That is so.'

'Tell me, doctor. During the four days before John Wilcox's death did you at any time have reason to believe that Miss Gray had a pistol in her possession?'

'Certainly not.'

'My learned friend will suggest to you, no doubt, that it might have been concealed in her handbag.'

'It was a large one, certainly, and generally very full, as women's handbags tend to be.'

'No room for a gun, you think?'

'I think not. I think I should have noticed that she handled it differently if there had been anything so heavy in it.'

'Thank you, doctor.' He smiled, as Halloran came to his feet with clumsy speed. 'Here is my friend with some more questions for you,' he said, and sat down.

'I think you will agree with me,' Halloran began, 'that no kind of surveillance was ever practised upon Miss Gray in your household, at least since she grew up.'

'Of course not.' The witness sounded indignant.

'Then the task of secreting a gun, even so large a one as a Mauser automatic pistol, would not have been beyond her.'

'I don't know.' Now he was doubtful. 'I still think it would have been too difficult.'

'You remember the evening of the eleventh of November, doctor?'

'Vividly.'

'Will you tell us—?'

'I had no surgery that evening, and for a wonder no patients to visit either. We were having a drink before dinner, my wife and I, when Ellen came in with what I can only describe as a very determined manner. She said, "I've been wanting to corner you, Uncle," and proceeded to ask me about her father's trial.'

'Did she tell you she had come to believe in his innocence?'

'Yes, she said that. Something about a poem, nonsense really. I didn't take any notice of it.'

'But she may have taken it seriously?'

'Oh, yes, I think she did.'

'So you told her—'

'As much as I could remember about the trial. Well, there wasn't any evidence for the defence except Edward's denial; in any case, I think I should have been more concerned to stress the points for the prosecution, because I considered her state of mind unhealthy.'

Maitland looked up, glanced at the judge, but then said nothing. 'In what way?' Halloran asked.

'Because there had never been any real doubt about her father's guilt, and I thought she should accept that,' said the witness reluctantly.

'And among the points for the prosecution that you mentioned, there was John Wilcox's evidence.'

'Yes. I suppose it struck her especially because she knew him so well.'

'What did she do?'

'She said, "Then it was his fault", and rushed out of the room; and very shortly I heard her leave the house.'

'Had she been upstairs?'

'Yes. But she wasn't up there more than a minute.'

'Now, would you say the accused has an even temper?'

The witness hesitated. 'I should say she has a quick temper,' he said at last, 'but just as quickly over.'

'What you told her of John Wilcox's part in her father's trial occasioned some loss of temper, did it not?'

'Yes, I'm afraid I must agree to that.'

'In fact, as she admits herself—'

'My lord!' said Maitland, on his feet again. 'My learned friend objected when I put portions of my client's statement to one of his witnesses.'

'You know perfectly well, Mr Maitland,' said the judge imperturbably, 'the basis on which that objection rested. I find Mr Halloran in order.'

'As your lordship pleases.' He sat down again and began to doodle on the back of his brief, scoring the thick paper with bold, savage strokes. Halloran had needed no further invitation to proceed.

'Would you agree that the accused, as she says herself, was very angry?'

'I have to agree to that,' said the witness, sounding unhappy.

'And do you think, all things considered, doctor, that that was a reasonable reaction to what you had told her?'

'I thought she reacted in an exaggerated way. I could not see myself that what John – what Mr Wilcox had done was so very bad.'

Halloran opened his mouth to speak, glanced at Maitland, who seemed to be simmering on the verge of another objection, and changed his mind about what he had been going to say. 'Thank you, doctor,' he said instead. Maitland was on his feet almost before the words were out of his mouth.

'When you spoke of my client as having a quick temper, you also said that it was quickly over. Do you think her "very angry" state would have lasted even as long as it took her to get to Bayswater?'

'No, that would have given her time to cool down.'

'Her journey included, according to her own statement, a walk across the park. A further soothing influence ... don't you think?'

'Yes, certainly,' said the witness, looking happier than he had done for some time. And was allowed to take his leave.

The housekeeper and the charwoman. Maitland had known their names, of course, but hardly bothered to remember them. It was negative evidence at best, that no gun had been seen in Ellen's possession. It was no part of their duties to rummage through her belongings, as Halloran's junior didn't fail to point out during the course of a rather perfunctory cross-examination. The defence saw them go without regret.

Stephen Langland was next, and here Maitland was aroused to more interest. The man who wasn't exactly engaged to Ellen Gray, at least according to her version of the affair. Speaking to his brief, that was the first question he put to the witness after the preliminaries were over. 'You are a good friend of Miss Gray's?'

'More than that, I'm going to marry her.' He was a slightly built man, not much taller than Ellen herself, if Maitland was any judge. His hair was darkish, his eyes dark too, probably brown, and he had a direct way of looking and speaking that was immediately pleasing. He made the statement, not belligerently but quite firmly, obviously intending to be believed. Which might be a good thing, if it made the jury feel sympathetic towards the defendant. On the other hand ...

'My friend, Mr Halloran, will suggest to you in due course that you are lying because you are in love with Ellen Gray.'

That was a gamble, of course, but miraculously it came off. 'I happen to be a churchgoer,' said Langland, not quite so easily now, but still convincingly enough. 'I wouldn't say anything on oath that I didn't mean.'

'Thank you.' Counsel's gratitude was quite sincere. 'There is the question of the Hand-gun Club to which you both belonged. Did you join at the same time?'

'No. I had been a member for some years.'

'How did it come about that Miss Gray joined too?'

'She didn't. She came a few times as my guest.'

'How many times, can you remember?'

'I think, four.'

'And what progress did she make in the art of target shooting?'

'Not much. She wasn't very good. I think her interest was – was academic rather than practical.'

'I see. Now there is the question of your visit to the club on the seventh November. You went together on that occasion, I believe.'

'We did.'

'Did you hear any talk of a Mauser automatic pistol that the secretary had been given?'

'I did hear it mentioned. I don't think Ellen was with me at the time though.'

'Where was she?'

'Shooting at the range.'

'Did you mention the matter to her when you were together again?'

'Not that I remember. I can't be positive, but I wasn't very interested.'

'Were you together all the evening?'

'Yes.'

'She didn't absent herself from you for any reason at all?'

'No. I'm quite sure about that.'

'Thank you, Mr Langland. That is all I wanted to ask you.'

Halloran came to his feet slowly. Not a deliberate attempt, Maitland thought, at intimidation, but impressive all the same. 'Now, Mr Langland, I heard what you told my friend. You are a sincere man, sincerely trying to tell the truth. But can you deny that – subconsciously perhaps – you are slanting the truth in the prisoner's favour?'

'I have answered all the questions as accurately as I could.'

'And you are telling us, you are maintaining, that Miss Gray could not have taken the gun without your knowledge.'

'That is my position, yes.'

'She was in your sight the whole time you were at the club—'

86

'Yes.'

'—even when you were shooting.'

If it hadn't dismayed him so much, Maitland would have found Langland's look of dismay positively ludicrous. He stammered, 'Of c-course not.' And then, rallying a little, 'But it wasn't—'

'That was the purpose of your visit to the club, was it not? To shoot?' said Halloran inexorably.

'Yes, but—'

'There is no need for excuses.' Halloran's tone was kindly, almost fatherly. 'The jury will know what weight to put on your protestations,' he added, and seated himself with a distinct look of satisfaction.

Maitland hesitated only a moment before he said, 'No more questions.' The chap was shaken already, the chances were that between them they'd only make bad worse. It was a pity, for all that, but he should have foreseen it, of course. A campaigner of Halloran's experience ...

And after that there were just the two character witnesses. A gesture, no more. He wasn't really relying on their evidence at all, but you had to go through the motions and Horton had dug them up with commendable zeal.

Frederick Wentworth Tate, Engineer by profession, Technical Director of that old-established firm, Hitchcock's. Maitland studied him carefully, thinking of all the questions he would have liked to ask, purely out of curiosity, about Edward Gray, and his wife, and his wife's lover. Tate was a tall, bulky man with a high-domed forehead under a receding hair line. He looked quite self-possessed, and seemed to be trying to catch the prisoner's eye, but she kept her head resolutely bent and looked at no-one. Again Maitland thought what a lonely figure she made, as if all the world had abandoned her. Perhaps he should have seen her again, made a greater effort to bring her to his way of thinking. But it was too late for that now, and here was Frederick Tate, who looked a cheerful, friendly man, whom his friends would undoubtedly call Fred, waiting for his questions.

And, of course, there was nothing new, nothing beyond his proof. Ellen Gray had a quiet, kindly nature, the last person in the world to injure another. And he had never seen any signs of ill temper in her. Halloran pressed him about that, when it came to his turn, but there was no shaking him. Anyone would have been forgiven for thinking, thought Maitland a little sourly, that the prisoner was a candidate for immediate beatification. Somehow he didn't like the picture that Tate's determined charity conjured up, but perhaps it would be to the jury's taste.

So then there was Martin John Roydon, who promised to be just as bad, just as unreal in his assessment of what after all was a flesh and blood woman, not a lay figure to be described in a few easy words. Martin Roydon was a Chartered Accountant, lived at Streatham, was Chief Accountant to the local firm of Willoughby, Spencer and Company, wholesale stationers. He was almost as tall as Tate, but of much narrower build. A careful, precise man, from the looks of him. He, too, thought Ellen Gray was unlikely to react with violence to any situation whatever, though when it came to the point he didn't deny she had a temper. A quick one, quickly over, it certainly wouldn't have survived a bus ride to town and a walk across the park. Halloran did what he could with that, and Roydon was so cautious in his answers that any good he might have done was certainly discounted. Maitland watched him go without regret, and was conscious of a distinct feeling of relief when he realised that the judge was about to adjourn. He'd have the chance to polish up his closing remarks tonight.

III

'I imagine you are under the impression,' said Sir Nicholas that evening, 'that your performance in court today advanced your client's case in some way.' He was a man as tall as his nephew, though rather more heavily built, with fair hair in which the grey hardly showed, and an authoritative manner of which he was quite unconscious; and he had arrived with the coffee cups, for the express purpose of being controversial, or so Maitland thought. Antony himself was feeling tired, and more conscious than usual of the pain in his shoulder (a legacy of the war), and would have been glad enough to be spared anything in the nature of an argument.

He didn't pretend, however, not to know what his uncle meant. Only he was puzzled. 'I never could get along with Conway,' he said. 'But how did you hear about it so quickly, Uncle Nick?'

'Why, from Halloran, of course. He was on the telephone soon after I got home. Amused, naturally, and inclined to be pleased with himself.'

'Yes, well, he has good cause to be,' said Antony honestly. 'Everything's running his way.'

To his surprise, Sir Nicholas did not press the matter beyond that point, except to say, 'I wonder,' in rather a pensive tone. Instead, after complaining to Jenny in rather a perfunctory way that his coffee cup was not filled to the precise point which met with his approval, he went on to talk of other things, and the evening passed harmoniously. Antony, putting the final polish on his closing speech for the defence after the others had retired, had a thought to spare for his uncle's uncharacteristic behaviour. But it was an unprofitable field of speculation, and after a moment or two he dismissed it from his mind.

FRIDAY, the third day of the trial

He delivered himself of the address the next morning, without any great hope that the jury would pay heed to it. He made his points carefully, of course, hammered them home as well as he could, because if the jury had caught them in passing as the trial proceeded they had certainly forgotten them by now. The lack of motive ... in particular the lack of motive at the time the pistol was alleged to have been stolen. The absence of any suggestion that Ellen Gray could have owned a weapon such as the one used, let alone used it efficiently. The disagreement between two of the prosecution's witnesses as to the time that had elapsed between their hearing the shot and finding his client with the murdered man. The evidence of the accused's good character ... a case where you had to rely on that sort of thing was as good as lost already.

Halloran's own closing speech was interrupted by the luncheon recess, but it would have taken more than that to put him off his stride. Maitland hardly heard the rounded phrases, he could have spun the whole thing out of his head, without notes, himself. The judge's summing-up ... well, he could have recited that too. Scrupulously fair, that was Carruthers's way, every point weighed carefully and given its due value.

He took the opportunity of studying the prisoner again while Carruthers was speaking. It was quite safe to do so, she never raised her head. He thought angrily, 'She should have let us have our way.' But the anger didn't go very deep. The trial had – had diminished her. He couldn't describe it any other way. She was no longer the lively, self-possessed girl he had interviewed at the prison, but a woman grown old before her time, and shrunk in upon herself somehow, as though there was nowhere in the world she could look for a ray of hope. That being so, the thought of what the years in prison would do depressed him. Even if she was guilty ... he caught himself up on the thought, there could be no doubt about that. But even so, she had had more than her share of sorrow in her life already.

But he needn't have worried. The jury deliberated for precisely forty minutes, and came back to return a verdict of Not Guilty.

'I understand you are to be congratulated,' said Sir Nicholas cordially. Roger Farrell had already arrived when he came upstairs that evening, and Jenny had to fetch another coffee cup.

Antony thought, Halloran again! and was suspicious of the cordiality. 'It was a completely unexpected verdict,' he said cautiously.

'But not by Uncle Nick.' Jenny was filling the cup more carefully this evening, to precisely one quarter of an inch from the top. 'He knew all the time, didn't you?' she added, passing the cup.

'Let's say, I wasn't altogether surprised.'

'You couldn't have known!' Antony sounded outraged. And then, when his uncle only smiled and shook his head at him, added rudely, 'If you're going to set up as a ruddy clairvoyant—'

'You're exaggerating, my dear boy, as you so often do. I had the advantage of hearing from Halloran from time to time, as well as the newspaper reports.'

'He must have been remarkably communicative then,' said Roger. 'The reports themselves didn't tell me much.'

'No, and anyway it's ridiculous,' said Antony. 'Everything was going his way. Really it was,' he went on, looking round as though someone had disagreed with him.

'I don't think you allow sufficiently for your own eloquence in a cause you believe in,' said Sir Nicholas, with intent to annoy. Antony would have said, with some truth, that his uncle was the orator in the family.

'You know perfectly well—'

'One of your damned crusades, somebody called them. Was it Horton? In any event it's an apt phrase. Once your crusading spirit takes over—'

'I did not believe her innocent,' said Antony, spacing out each word to give it greater emphasis. 'You know yourself, Uncle Nick, I tried to get her to plead "Not Guilty by reason of diminished responsibility" and let us do what we could with that. I shouldn't have done that if I'd believed her.'

'You don't know your own strength, my boy,' said Sir Nicholas unkindly.

Roger and Jenny exchanged a resigned look. Jenny went away to fetch cognac and glasses, while Roger flung himself into the breach. 'I don't see what there is to get worked up about, Antony,' he said. 'It's surely a compliment—'

Antony grinned. 'If it was meant that way,' he said, more cheerfully. 'But I do assure you, Uncle Nick—'

'Yes, I know what you are going to say. You may believe it yourself, for all I know. But I'll make a small bet with you, Roger. Before the month's out he will be actively engaged in proving Ellen Gray's innocence to her family and friends by unmasking the real murderer.'

'Done!' said Roger. Antony scowled at him. 'May I ask you something, Uncle Nick?' Roger went on. 'Do *you* believe the Not Guilty verdict was the right one?'

'Of course I don't, being a reasonable man. But once Antony gets an idea in his head—'

'I do not think she is innocent,' said Antony, a little too loudly. 'And that's my last word on the subject.' Nor would he consent to be any further drawn.

But he returned to the matter without prompting when he and Jenny were alone together, after the visitors had gone. 'I really meant what I said about thinking that wretched girl guilty, you know.'

'I'm sure you did.' If there was a hint of the demure in Jenny's tone, it was too slight for him to take offence. 'So Uncle Nick will lose his bet.'

'Of course he will.' He paused a moment, and then added rather hesitantly, 'What I can't get out of my head, love, is the feeling that perhaps, after all, Edward Gray might have been innocent.'

'Ellen's father? Oh, but, Antony—'

'Nothing to be done about it now. I know that. But the few lines of verse that started the whole thing keep going through my mind. Sentimental ... maudlin ... but if she meant what she said—'

'You're arguing as you say Ellen argued.'

'No harm in that. If Madeleine Gray wrote that – that drivel, and meant it, she'd hardly have been carrying on with another man six months later. Or would she?'

'If she was really in love with Edward—'

'We're saying that she was.'

'Well, in that case, six months wasn't very long to get over it. Especially as he was only missing, she didn't know he was dead.'

'He wasn't.'

'No, of course not. But what I meant—'

'I know what you meant,' said Antony, rather hastily. Jenny's explanations were apt to become unduly involved. 'Well, in that case we're left with the supposition that Edward Gray jumped to the wrong conclusion, merely from seeing his wife with another man, which – unless he was a raving lunatic – just isn't likely.'

'We don't know what happened to him during the six months he was missing.'

'His sufferings might have driven him mad? Well, if so, he did a pretty good job of concealing the fact, didn't he? There was never any suggestion—'

'I'm willing to agree with you, if it will make you

94

feel any better,' said Jenny, when he broke off, looking suddenly thoughtful. 'But it wasn't your case, so I don't see why you're worrying, and there's nothing to be done about it now.'

'No,' said Antony, but clearly he wasn't attending. 'I wonder who did appear for the defence,' he added, after a pause.

'Oh, Antony!' said Jenny, exasperated.

PART THREE

HILARY TERM
(continued)

1965

SUNDAY, 31st January

I

In the event, Sir Nicholas almost lost his bet, because
it was not until the last day of the month that Stephen
Langland turned up in Kempenfeldt Square. He arrived
just as they were finishing tea upstairs, and when Gibbs
had toiled up to announce the visitor Sir Nicholas was
immediately on the alert. 'Langland,' he said. 'I seem to
remember that name.'

Antony was on his feet. 'He's the man who may or
may not be engaged to Ellen Gray,' he said.

'Come now, it must be one thing or the other.'

'He says, Yes. She says, No. In any case—'

'You will notice that I am carefully refraining from
saying, I told you so,' Sir Nicholas pointed out. Antony
took one last gulp of tea, and grinned at him.

'If you're thinking of your bet with Roger, I wouldn't
be too sure yet you've won it,' he said. 'I take it you've
no objection to my using the study for a while, Uncle
Nick.'

'In the circumstances, you have my blessing,' said Sir
Nicholas, at his mellowest. Antony exchanged a look with
Jenny, half amused, half exasperated, and went out of
the room.

As he went downstairs he reflected that he wasn't
really surprised by the visit, only that it was Langland,
rather than Doctor Clive, who had come. But it was awkward to have to refuse the help that was surely going to
be asked. It wasn't much fun being tried for murder,

even if you were acquitted, and the after effects were apt to be unexpectedly distressing; as things were Ellen Gray and her friends should be thankful, he thought, for small mercies. But it would be too cruel, perhaps, to say that openly.

He found himself, when he joined Langland in the study, a little surprised at the visitor's appearance, and this was no unfamiliar emotion. In the witness box, Stephen had been neat to the point of dandyism, now he wore old tweeds and a much more relaxed air. At least, that was what Antony thought until he got a good look at him.

He was saying the usual things. '... good of you to see me. I ought to have phoned, but I thought you might refuse out of hand, and then I should have been stymied.'

'You'd better reserve your gratitude, you may find it isn't needed,' said Antony. Better begin, he thought, as he meant to go on. 'But sit down, Mr Langland, and tell me what I can do for you.'

'Thank you.' There was a pause while they seated themselves and openly took stock of each other. Then Stephen said, 'You look different without your wig, you know, but I don't think that's the only difference. I came because I've heard of you, that sometimes you've been able to help people in a similar situation to Ellen's, but I think, after all, it may not be too difficult talking to you.'

'I don't bite,' said Antony a little tartly, because he hated to be reminded of the publicity that had attended some of his cases. Then, when Stephen did not immediately respond, he added, 'You said, "a situation similar to Ellen's", Mr Langland. Could you explain to me what you mean by that.'

'Well ... well ... she feels that nobody believes the jury's verdict, Mr Maitland.'

'You, yourself—'

'I believe in her, of course.' It was at that moment that Antony realised that the air of relaxation was carefully assumed, as carefully perhaps as had been the calmness with which he gave evidence. Stephen wasn't relaxed at all, he was strung up to the highest pitch of nervous tension. But perhaps he believed what he said.

'I see. But I don't quite see how it concerns me, you know. My part was played in court.'

'Yes, I – we're all grateful for that. But if you could see your way to looking a bit further into the matter—'

Maitland got to his feet. He did not realise that his own mood almost duplicated the other man's, but he felt a quite inescapable need to move about the room. 'I don't think I can help you,' he said.

'Don't say that! It's really ... if you'll listen to me, Mr Maitland, I'll try to explain.'

'I'll listen, of course. But don't count on anything, because—'

Stephen, it seemed, had only heard the first part of that. He interrupted eagerly. 'I don't think you realise – how could you? – just what the trial did to Ellen. She's completely changed. She's nervous, hates meeting people—'

'Are you telling me she's become a recluse?'

'No, nothing like that. She doesn't give way to her feelings, she's back at work and even talking about changing her job. But the strain is terrific.'

'A doctor—'

'There's Doctor Clive. He did call in his partner to see her, and he prescribed something to make her sleep. But that isn't what she needs, Mr Maitland, she needs to know that people believe in her. And I don't see how she can ever feel that until the real murderer is exposed.'

'That's easier said than done.' He ought to add more, to be more explicit about his own feelings, but there was the unwanted tug of sympathy that had betrayed him so often in the past. This time the circumstances were different, and he heard Langland's next words like an echo of his own thoughts.

'*You* don't believe her.'

'You must understand, Mr Langland, that it is no part of counsel's duty—'

'But I was in court after I gave my evidence. It didn't sound like that. You fought as though you believed every word you said.'

'I—'

'Don't you think she deserves a chance? There was that business of her father to face in her childhood, and now this. It's more than one person should be asked to bear.'

'Tell me something, Mr Langland. Does Miss Gray know that you are here?'

'I told her I was coming. She said it was no use. I didn't – I didn't want to believe her.'

'Are you still engaged to be married?'

'No. Ellen won't. She says she'd only be a drag on me.'

'And that's why—'

'That's one of the reasons. A completely selfish one, as no doubt you're going to point out. But even if she never agrees – I mean this, Mr Maitland – I still want her to be happy.'

'Yes, I'm sure you do. Tell me something, Mr Langland. What do you think of the case of Edward Gray?'

Stephen stared at him for a moment. 'Why, I – what the hell does that matter now?'

'It might matter a great deal.' For a moment he halted his pacing. 'You're right in thinking I believe Miss Gray guilty, Mr Langland, but when I think about her father's case I'm not altogether sure in my own mind that he was.'

'But it doesn't matter one way or the other. Certainly not to me.'

'I shouldn't be in too much of a hurry to say that. For one thing, it means a great deal to Miss Gray. That was the start of all the trouble, wasn't it?'

'Yes, I suppose so. But I don't see what you're getting at.'

'I am willing to make some attempt to do what you want,' – now, what in the world had possessed him to say that, just as though he had meant to from the beginning – 'that is, to work for a while on the assumption of Miss Gray's innocence, which is the only way I can proceed. Who knows? I may come around to your way of thinking.'

Stephen was on his feet too, and he was frowning. 'It isn't exactly—' he said.

'I'm afraid I must say, take it or leave it.'

'Then I'll take it, of course . . . and with gratitude.'

'I told you to wait a while for that. You realise – don't you? – that I can only proceed in this matter so far as her family and friends allow me—'

'Yes.'

'—and that I'm not likely to be popular with any of them, or even with Miss Gray herself, by the time I've finished.'

'I'm sure—'

'It's all very well for you, Mr Langland. You can't be said to be one of the inner circle.'

'I'm very concerned.'

'Yes, oh yes.' Antony interrupted him again. 'But did you know the dead man, for instance? Did you know John Wilcox?'

'I had met most of Ellen's friends during the past year.'

'Who were they?'

'That's rather a big question,' said Stephen, taken aback.

'Yes, you'd better sit down again. But it was your idea to start this, Mr Langland.'

'Well, there were the people I met at the tennis club, Barbara and Roy Wilcox among them, though I think they came as Ellen's guests, they weren't members. I suppose Ellen's closest friends—'

'I may be able to spare you some trouble. Were any of these people old enough to have known her parents?'

'What can that have to do with it?'

'Don't worry your head about that, I have to go my own way, I'm afraid.'

'Most of them would be my age – early thirties – or Ellen's age, or younger. Of those who were older, we joined up with Madge and Everard Carter once or twice for dinner. They were certainly of an age to have known Mr and Mrs Gray, but nothing in the conversation led me to think they had done so.'

Maitland had halted his pacing, produced the inevitable envelope, and gone over to the desk to write. 'Let's leave the tennis club then,' he suggested.

'I've already told you I'd met John Wilcox and his wife.'

'Frances?' said Maitland, still scribbling.

'That's right. Ellen was at home with them as she would have been with her own family.'

'As she was with Doctor and Mrs Clive?'

'Pretty well. Only she was grateful to the Clives too, and that complicated the relationship, I think.'

'I see. What do you think of Ellen's temper?'

The sudden question threw Stephen into a state of indecision. 'I—' he began, and broke off, looking about him rather wildly, as though he might draw inspiration in some way from the comfortable furnishings of Sir Nicholas's favourite room.

Antony waited a moment and then said quietly, 'I can't help you unless you tell me the truth.'

'Well, you may think ... she's got a temper all right,'

said Stephen reluctantly. 'But it's quickly over, she couldn't possibly—'

'What she heard on the eleventh of November last was something that concerned her very deeply.'

'Yes, I suppose so. But you can argue it any way you like, I still won't believe you.'

'Never mind.' He came to stand on the hearthrug, and bent to stir the fire, which was burning sluggishly. When he straightened again he turned and smiled down at his companion. 'That's either sticking to your principles or sheer stubbornness, according to which way you look at it. Tell me about Miss Gray's other friends.'

'If you want the ones who knew her parents, there were the two chaps who gave character evidence at the trial.'

'Frederick Tate. How did he get on with Ellen?'

'Very well. I should think he gets on well with everybody, a very likeable chap.'

'That's how he struck me, certainly. What about his wife, whose name, if I remember correctly, is Mathilda?'

'Matty, they call her. She's one of those unflappable people, never at a loss. Which is just as well, because they have five children, and I don't think the oldest is more than ten. She always struck me as being rather fond of Ellen, but she wasn't married until after the war, she didn't know her parents.'

'That leaves the other fellow, then.' He fished another envelope out of his pocket, but did not consult it. 'Martin Roydon,' he said.

'Oh, he's a different kettle of fish altogether. Polite enough, but not easy to know. He did his best for Ellen though, didn't he? That makes him all right in my book.'

'He, too, knew Edward and Madeleine Gray, but his wife – Dorothy – didn't.'

'Well, I wouldn't be sure about that because, as I say, conversation didn't always flow easily. Dorothy is good fun when you get her alone, but inclined to be quiet when her husband is present. I don't know there is really much more I can tell you about them.'

'Let's call it a day then. Unless ... what do you think Ellen would have done if she'd arrived in Bayswater to find John Wilcox still alive?'

'Stormed at him, I suppose, and then quieted down, let him have his say, and forgiven him.'

'In other words, her ill temper would have survived the journey from Roehampton.'

'I didn't say that. But you must remember she'd gone there specifically to have things out with him.'

'I'm not forgetting it. But it doesn't make the task you've given me any easier, does it?'

For the first time, Langland smiled. 'Everybody talks nowadays about things being a challenge,' he said. 'Perhaps it's you who should be grateful to me.'

II

When he had seen the visitor out, about ten minutes later, Antony hesitated a moment before he began to climb the stairs. There wasn't much chance of explaining to Uncle Nick how he had come to agree to Langland's request without in the slightest degree believing the premise on which he must work.

And it was just as he had thought. 'I could have told you how it would be,' said Sir Nicholas. 'You've persuaded yourself of the woman's innocence.'

'I have not. I only said—'

'If that is true, Antony,' said Sir Nicholas, with the maddening assumption that he could read his nephew's mind, '– and you may think it is, though I have my doubts – it only renders the matter still more inexplicable. To use valuable time on a wild goose chase—'

'It's my own time, Uncle Nick.'

'So I should hope. May I remind you that our profession is one that demands a certain amount of concentration from its members, and this – this investigation, to dignify it with a respectable sounding title, is not one that can be supposed in any way to further your career. You should never have consented.'

'I was trying to win your bet for you.' But that wasn't a popular remark either. They were still arguing – half-heartedly on Antony's part – when Roger and Meg arrived at six o'clock.

'You should have known better than to gamble against the likelihood of any idiocy on my nephew's part,' said Sir Nicholas by way of greeting.

III

Fortunately, perhaps, he had another engagement, and wasn't staying to dinner. Roger was laughing when Antony came back into the room after seeing his uncle out. 'I must say, as he describes it, it does sound pretty harebrained,' he said.

Antony gave him a sour look. 'Don't you start,' he said. 'I've had quite enough of the subject for one evening.'

'But do you really still think she's guilty?' Meg was quite oblivious of storm clouds.

'*I* think so. But who's to say I'm right. And if I'm wrong—'

'I'm beginning to see,' said Jenny, but Meg was more bracing.

'It seems to me you've done pretty well by her, whichever way you look at it,' she said.

'In certain circumstances that might not be enough.'

'You mean, if she's innocent.'

'Precisely.'

'Don't *say* that, darling,' said Meg. 'You sound just like Uncle Nick. And it seems to me you haven't been telling him all the truth. If you're beginning to have doubts—'

'I didn't say that. But even if it was true, Meg, it wouldn't be good for him to let him think he'd been right from the beginning.'

'No, I see that, of course,' she agreed seriously.

'I thought you might.' Antony got up, refilled glasses all round, and went back to his favourite place on the hearth-rug. 'Do you happen to have known John Wilcox, Roger? He was a stock-broker too, I understand.'

'Yes, I knew him quite well.'

'Darling, why ever didn't you tell me that?' Meg demanded.

'It didn't seem a very interesting item of information.'

'But someone who'd been murdered! Of course it was interesting. Wasn't it, Jenny?'

'I suppose so. I don't like mysteries,' said Jenny.

'Well, but—'

'Let's say I didn't want to encourage the morbid streak in you,' said Roger. Meg relapsed into an indignant silence. 'If you want to know what I thought of him,' he added, looking up at Antony, 'he was a pretty sound fellow.'

'No scandals?'

'No.'

'No rivals gunning for him?'

'You seem to have a pretty distorted notion of life on the stock exchange,' said Roger, amused. 'No, I don't think anyone was gunning for him. As I meant to convey, he had the highest reputation.'

'Did he work alone?'

'No, he was a member of one of the big firms, Rogers, Meldrum and Stevens. A director for the past eight or nine years. But I don't think – well, it's only an opinion,

108

Antony – that anyone was likely to murder him because of his business affairs.'

'Not the sort of person either to be a double murderer?'

'*Now* what have you got into your head?' Roger enquired; and in almost the same moment Jenny exclaimed, 'Oh, dear!' and Meg – whose sulks never lasted for long – said brightly, 'I told you it was interesting, darlings.'

Antony looked from one of them to the other. 'To take those remarks in order,' he said, 'my day will not have been wasted, *darling*, if I have contrived to interest you. As for you, Jenny, I'm not quite sure—'

'You're trying to tie in that old murder, you don't know *what* you may uncover,' she said.

'You're right, of course, but it can't do any harm, love,' he told her. 'I'll explain my ideas about that in a minute. As for you, Roger, Jenny's answered your question for you, hasn't she?'

'I suppose so, but I don't see the connection between the two cases, I'm afraid.'

'Then listen. You can argue the matter two ways.'

'Only two,' said Meg hopefully. Antony smiled at her.

'Two will do to be going on with,' he said. 'You have assured me, Roger, that it is unlikely that Wilcox had business enemies. And in my enquiries I keep coming across the same group of people, who seem to be close friends: William and Alison Clive – he was Ellen's guardian while she was growing up; John and Frances Wilcox; Martin and Dorothy Roydon; and Frederick and Mathilda Tate. If Ellen is innocent, and I am working on that assumption for the moment, it seems likely that one of these people is guilty.'

'Wait a bit! That's the devil of an assumption to make. Wilcox must have had dozens of friends.'

'All right, let's start from the other end. Jenny knows my reasons, and I think she agrees with me in wondering whether Edward Gray was guilty after all.'

Meg said, 'There now!' Jenny picked up her glass and sipped sherry thoughtfully. Roger said nothing either, but his look of interest quickened.

'If that is so – yes, I know it's only a hypothesis – the same tight little group of people appear as suspects, all close friends of Edward and Madeleine Gray, and of Michael Foster too, I suppose.'

'According to that, if someone murders you, Antony, Meg and I shall be the chief suspects.'

'No, because . . . you'll know the answer if you think for a minute.'

'You've led a rackety sort of life—'

'I won't agree to that, but I think you've got my meaning.'

'—whereas Mrs Gray lived quietly at home with her daughter, in her husband's absence with the army.'

'Prec – oh, well, exactly, if you prefer it, Meg. That should mean someone had a personal motive, shouldn't it?'

'That points to her husband.'

'No, because we've agreed – Jenny and I have agreed – that perhaps he didn't have a motive after all. Unless Madeleine was unfaithful to him—'

'And you have reason to doubt that?'

'The same reason that Ellen had. The few lines of verse that her mother had scribbled on the fly-leaf of a book.'

> 'I only know that my heart is sore,
> And my eyes are blind with tears,
> As I turn from the path I may not tread
> And face the lonely years,'

said Meg, surprising them all. Antony gave her a grin. 'Fancy you remembering that.'

'I read it in the newspaper. I always was a quick study.'

'Well, I admit, recited by you it doesn't sound so very bad. But for all its faults I can't help feeling there's some genuine emotion there.'

'All right then,' said Roger, 'we'll acquit Edward Gray. What follows?'

'A personal motive, one of the same group of people. My point is that if one of them murdered Madeleine it's rather a coincidence if Ellen turned out to be a murderer too. For that matter, it's the hell of a coincidence if both Edward and Ellen were murderers ... don't you think?'

'It's an argument, certainly,' said Roger, thinking it out, 'but I don't know that it convinces me.'

'Well, it's the only possible theory for me to work on, if I'm to do anything at all. One group of people, one murderer. Not Edward, because he died in 1956. Not Ellen, because she was only eight years old in 1945.'

'But you said—'

'I've got to have some starting point, Meg, and this is it.'

'Well, I think it all sounds too terribly plausible, darling.'

'A working hypothesis,' said Roger, still thoughtfully. 'I see your point, Antony, but—'

'It's no good saying "but",' Jenny told him. 'You can see he's made up his mind. And Uncle Nick was bad enough on the subject,' she added reflectively, 'but I wonder what Inspector Conway will say when he hears you've opened the case again.'

'We won't even think about that,' said Antony firmly. All the same the conversation, all that evening, had a habit of drifting back to the same subject, without anything very constructive being said.

WEDNESDAY, 3rd February

I

It was a couple of days before he found himself with any time on his hands, but when he phoned William Clive he was lucky enough to find the doctor enjoying one of his rare days of rest. 'I've been expecting you,' he said, more resigned than anything else, if one could judge from his tone. 'This afternoon will do quite well. Yes, about four o'clock. I'll be looking out for you.'

'Will Miss Gray be at home?'

'Do you want her?'

'If possible.'

'Then I'll get her to phone Stephen and ask for the afternoon off. There shouldn't be any difficulty, in view of the fact—' He broke off there, though without leaving Maitland in much doubt as to how the sentence should have ended. Again judging from his tone, Doctor Clive didn't sound any too pleased with the turn events had taken.

But that guess was only half right, as he soon found out when he arrived at the house in Roehampton Lane that afternoon. Doctor Clive and his wife awaited him in the drawing-room, and the doctor began to speak almost before the first greetings were over.

'Don't misunderstand me, Mr Maitland, I'm delighted – we're both delighted that you can see your way to looking into Ellen's case a little further. But Stephen hinted that you were thinking of tying it in with that old affair of Edward's, and that's quite another matter.'

Langland, then, had a sensitive ear, to catch the nuances of something that had been by no means clearly expressed. 'You don't approve?' Antony asked.

'Most certainly I do not. It's unsettling for Ellen, and no good can possibly come of it.'

'You don't think then that he might, after all, have been innocent?'

'There can be no question of it. You probably don't remember the case, Mr Maitland, it caused no great stir at the time, but the evidence was quite clear. There was no doubt of his guilt.'

'Do you agree with that, Mrs Clive?'

'Yes, oh yes. Indeed I do.' She laughed as she spoke, for no very apparent reason, but she seemed livelier than she had done at their first meeting, even inclined to chatter a little. 'I have to agree with my husband, you know. It wouldn't be kind to Ellen to encourage her to believe that old verdict might be reversed.'

'That's not exactly what I'm aiming at. I only feel that learning about one case may illuminate matters so far as the other is concerned.'

'Not at all kind,' repeated Mrs Clive, shaking her head.

What to say to that? You're leaving me without any prop for a rather shaky belief in your niece's innocence. 'Perhaps you would answer a few questions for me all the same,' he said.

'So long as you understand our position.' Doctor Clive sounded doubtful. 'Though I should prefer to have your assurance that you won't encourage Ellen in this un-reasonable attitude of hers.'

'I'm afraid I shall have nothing reassuring to say to her on either count. It's very doubtful – I explained this to Mr Langland – that I shall be able to do any good at all.'

'Well then, we must do what we can to help, mustn't

we, my dear? And hope that your pessimism isn't justified as far as Ellen is concerned.'

'Anything, anything at all,' said Mrs Clive, smiling at Antony seraphically.

He couldn't resist smiling back at her. 'You're glad about the verdict, aren't you?' he asked.

'So very, very glad. Grateful just to have Ellen home again,' she told him.

'I can understand that. Will you tell me something about Edward and Madeleine Gray,' he added, sharing the question between them.

'They'd been married for ten years, you know. They were – they always seemed ideally happy together.' That was the doctor.

'Ideally happy,' added his wife, emphasising the point.

'When Edward was posted as missing—?'

'Madeleine was heartbroken at the time. I'm sure that was genuine. But six months in war time, when everything changed so quickly—'

'Did you see much of her during that six months?'

'As much as time allowed. We were frantically busy then, with so many of the profession mobilised.'

'I was wondering—'

'I certainly noticed no change in her attitude. Did you, my dear?'

'No change at all.'

'Was Madeleine doing any war work?'

'She was an Air Raid Warden. There was a neighbour who would look after Ellen, even take her to and from school if necessary, when Madeleine was on duty.'

'They were never evacuated?'

'For a few weeks only, after Edward was called up. She missed her friends too much, she said. A lot of people did come back, you know, even when they had children.'

'So I have heard. There is the question of Michael Foster, then. Was he known to you?'

'I had met him once at the Grays' flat. I understood he was a friend of Edward's who, for one reason or another, was exempt from call-up. But that is all I know of him.'

'How did he strike you?'

'A pleasant enough young fellow. A little younger than the others, just as I was a little older. About Madeleine's age, I suppose.'

'The others?'

'Anyone who knew them will tell you that they always thought of Edward in connection with his three closest friends. Martin Roydon and Fred Tate, who gave evidence at the trial, and John Wilcox. They were at school together, something like that.'

'Until John Wilcox was killed, did those close ties still bind the surviving members of the group?'

'I can't say for sure—'

'—but they were certainly very close to Ellen, all of them,' Mrs Clive completed the sentence for him.

'Yes, that is true.'

'And Michael Foster was outside this – this inner circle?'

'As I was.'

'Did Madeleine ever speak of him?'

'As a friend who sometimes visited her. I never got any of the finer shades from her conversation, did you, my dear?'

'No,' said Mrs Clive, but she sounded doubtful. And then, smiling again, pleased to be able to help him, 'She did mention him rather a lot though, when I came to think about it afterwards.'

'You had no reason, though, to suspect any liaison between them?'

'Oh, no!' she said, succeeding in sounding both shocked and prim at the same time. 'Never anything like that.'

'You, doctor?'

'It came as a complete surprise to me.'

'Yet you accepted the prosecution's version of what happened without question.'

'I could so easily see Edward's angry reaction to anything that came upon him completely unawares. He was in the army, familiar with firearms. I am sorry to say this, Mr Maitland, but I can see it only too well.'

'And Ellen's temper is just as bad,' said Alison Clive, shaking her head sadly.

'But quickly over. You must admit that, my dear,' the doctor put in quickly.

'If you are both so certain, I suppose it is no use asking you if you have any other candidates for the role of murderer?'

'What motive could there have been? Madeleine lived very quietly, and though I know little of Foster, if someone had had a grudge against him they surely would not have waited until he was visiting a friend.'

'That's true, you know,' said Alison. 'Not what you wanted to hear,' she added, watching Maitland's expression.

'Of course I'd be glad of a short cut, but I can't say I was expecting one. Do you remember which branch of the service Edward was in?'

'In the Infantry. A company commander, in the Far East. I don't remember—'

'It doesn't matter. And when he was "missing, believed killed" do you know what had happened to him?'

'No. We never had any conversation with him after he came back, except when we were allowed to visit him in prison to talk about the arrangements for Ellen. It was hardly a time for reminiscences.'

'I can imagine that,' said Maitland, with feeling. Supposing this wild guess of his was right, and Edward Gray had indeed been innocent. The years he had spent

116

in prison ... it wasn't a nice thought. 'But I was wondering, you see, whether his experiences had been such as to render a plea of temporary insanity a reasonable one.'

'I always understood that he had refused to give any answer but a straight Not Guilty when he was charged.'

'That wasn't quite what I meant. If he had gone through a good deal this talk of a hair-trigger temper becomes more believable.'

'You're arguing against your own theory, Mr Maitland.'

'And shall again, no doubt. I only want the truth,' he said. And then, hopefully, 'What can you tell me about Frederick Tate and Martin Roydon?'

'Not much more than you learned at the trial.'

'You said – no, it was you, wasn't it, Mrs Clive? – that they were good friends of Ellen's. Doesn't that mean you knew them too?'

'Certainly I did, and regarded them as good friends myself, as I am sure my wife did.'

'Oh, yes, very good friends.'

'Then—'

'That means we found them pleasant, took pleasure in their company, not that we know anything that could be of interest to you.'

'Anything at all.'

'Well then, Fred is a contented, well adjusted man, happy in his work. Would you agree with that, my dear?'

'Very happy, and Matty so competent, the children so well behaved. If you want my opinion, Mr Maitland,' said Alison Clive thoughtfully, 'you need to have a placid disposition to be married to an extrovert.'

'Is that what he is?'

'No doubt about it at all.'

'And Martin Roydon?'

'Quite a different type.' Mrs Clive seemed to have taken over the answering now. 'You get the impression of hidden depths, if you know what I mean. And whether he likes his job or loathes it, I'm sure I don't know.'

'His wife?'

'Dorothy is a nonentity. I'm sorry to say that, but it's true, isn't it Will?'

'A little harsh, but not too much of an exaggeration.'

'Do they have any family?'

'Two sons, early teens. I don't know anything about them. They may be why Martin looks worried sometimes.'

'I see. What about the deceased ... John Wilcox?'

'John was a man with a passion for accuracy. He spent more than the other two, perhaps earned more. Certainly enjoyed good living. Frances is another worrier, I don't know what about.'

'The children?'

'I never heard of any trouble with them. Did you, Will?'

'No. Good, normal youngsters, as far as I know.'

'Thank you.' For some time Maitland had been suppressing a desire to get up and wander about the room, now he took the opportunity to get to his feet. 'I'm grateful for so much of your time,' he said. And then, 'Did Miss Gray stay home from work?'

'Yes, but reluctantly. She said she'd stay in her room unless you asked again for her.'

'I see. May I go up to her?'

'Use the dining-room, that will be more convenient.' Alison Clive was on her feet too. 'I'll fetch her to you, if you'll show him the way, Will.'

'Very well, my dear.' He smiled at Antony in what seemed for some reason to be a deprecating way, and Antony said, at random,

'Mrs Clive seems to be much better today.'

'She has her ups and downs. If you will come with me, Mr Maitland—'

The dining-room was unashamedly gloomy, with panelled walls and pictures of dead hares and pheasants and other appetite-inducing subjects hung above the panelling. Antony did not have to wait there long alone. He heard footsteps, and Alison Clive's voice apparently raised in encouragement, and then Ellen came in and shut the door firmly behind her, and stood looking at him, waiting for him to speak.

He waited a moment himself, taking in the change in her. No more than he might have expected from when he had seen her last in court, but the change from their first interview in the prison was very marked. She seemed – as he told it afterwards to Jenny – to have lost all spontaneity, to have become no more than a robot, badly programmed. Seen like this – he echoed his first impression of her – she no longer looked 'pretty stunning'. Without animation, her beauty repelled, rather than attracted. He said, on an impulse, 'Miss Gray, if you'd rather I didn't—'

'No.' Her voice was lifeless too, and when she added, 'Stephen tells me you're being kind enough to give me the benefit of the doubt,' you might have read some irony into the words, but none into the tone in which they were delivered.

'It amounts to that, yes.' That was said with deliberate brutality, but it didn't do anything to shake her out of her apathy. She said only, listlessly,

'For a moment in court, you know, I thought you believed what I told you. But if you didn't, I don't see why you're going to all the bother.'

'Let's say, because I gave Mr Langland my word. Apart from that, I made no promises, Miss Gray.'

'No,' she agreed. 'I'm not expecting anything, so you needn't be afraid of disappointing me.'

'Do you care even, either way? Or would you rather not be bothered?'

She paused to consider that, and for the first time a little colour came into her cheeks. 'If you feel I ought to be grateful to you, I'm sorry,' she said. 'I don't feel any gratitude, I'm afraid.'

'No reason why you should.' While they spoke she had seated herself at the head of the table, and after a moment's hesitation he took a chair on her left hand. 'I wish you'd tell me what's been happening, though,' he said. 'I could understand your being upset while you were still in prison, but now that you're free—'

'If you call it freedom.'

'What has happened?' he said again.

'Nothing that I shouldn't have expected, I suppose.'

'Phone calls?'

'Yes. You can't leave the phone unanswered in a doctor's house, you know, or even have the number changed. I don't take calls myself now, but I always know when there's been one because they upset Aunt Alison. And then there are letters. They can be burned, of course, but once you've read one you can imagine pretty well what the others will be like.'

'I see. I'm sorry. That will pass, you know.'

'So I suppose. But nothing will make people trust me again, Mr Maitland ... why should they?'

'Have you lost friends over this affair?'

'Funnily enough, none, so far as I know. Except the Wilcoxes, of course. Well, it hasn't been long, there are people I haven't seen yet. But life is full of conversations that break off when I approach, of people being too charming altogether, too kind.'

'You're letting your imagination run away with you.'

'That's easily said. Uncle Will tells me to pull myself together, and Stephen says I should forget everything that's happened. Only I don't see how I can.'

'Aren't you even interested any longer in proving your father's innocence?'

'Do you believe me about that?' It was the first, faint sign of interest she had shown.

'I think perhaps I do.'

'I see.' She might have been mimicking his own use of the words. 'But it isn't any use,' she added hopelessly. 'It's much too late to prove anything now.'

'Then let's tackle your problem.'

'I've told you so many times, Mr Maitland, what really happened.'

'There's one question you haven't answered, though. Did you see anyone on your way in whom you might have supposed to be coming from the Wilcoxes' flat?'

'I did answer that, Mr Maitland. There was nobody.'

'That was on second thoughts. Your first instinct was to prevaricate.'

'Now it's you who are making things up,' she retorted. But there was more life in her voice than there had been at any time that day.

'I don't think so. Miss Gray, if you saw anything, anything at all that might give me a lead—'

'But I didn't.' Her voice rose a little on the words. Maitland thought a little wryly what would be Sir Nicholas's comment on a colleague who took a witness from apathy to hysteria in one short interview. He pushed back his chair, therefore, and got to his feet.

'We'll leave it there, then. But if you change your mind—'

'I shan't. There's nothing to change it about,' she went on rather hurriedly, when he seemed about to speak again. 'Nothing I can tell you at all, Mr Maitland. Nothing, nothing, nothing!'

He didn't comment on that, said only, formally, 'Good-bye, Miss Gray.' She was still sitting at the table when he went out into the hall, taking with him the unsatisfactory feeling of unfinished business, and the equally unsatisfactory feeling that perhaps if he had chanced the hysterics and pressed a little harder something might have been accomplished. He wondered, too, if Stephen was one of the people who broke off conversations at Ellen's approach, and how, in her present state, she coped at all with her job as secretary. But that was something outside his terms of reference, and as he walked up the lane to the bus stop he dismissed it from his mind.

II

At dinner that evening he was eloquent upon the subject of his visit to Roehampton. Exceptionally, for a weekday, Roger had joined them for the meal, as Meg had some affair of her own that took her early to the theatre. It was odd, though – or perhaps not so odd – that neither he nor Jenny thought to point out the unreasonableness of Antony's attitude, though perhaps that was in Roger's mind when he asked, just as Jenny was serving the pudding, 'What does Geoffrey think of all this?'

Antony made a wide, extravagant gesture with his left hand, not suited to the dinner table. 'He's madly disapproving, and refuses to have anything to do with it.'

'Well, of course, Antony,' said Jenny, handing him a hot plate and forgetting to issue a warning, 'you couldn't really expect Geoffrey to be so – so unorthodox.'

'I didn't, don't worry. It's bad enough that I should be making a fool of myself,' he added bitterly. 'All the same, I'm sorry for that girl, even if she did kill John Wilcox.'

Jenny and Roger exchanged a glance. Perhaps neither of them was any longer believing this statement. 'You say she seems to have lost interest,' said Roger.

'Seems to have? I never saw anyone so uninterested. Even about her father, which I thought might rouse a spark considering her attitude before the trial, she doesn't seem to care any more.'

'This chap Langland. Does he really want to marry her, or does he want to get her off his conscience?' Roger asked.

'I think – but I wouldn't take any bets on it – that he really wants to marry her. But I'm probably making a fool of myself over that as well.'

'The jury agreed with you, over Ellen Gray at least.'

'They agreed with what I told them; or perhaps it was only that they didn't disagree with me,' said Antony thoughtfully.

'You convinced them by your sincerity,' said Jenny, hiding a smile. Antony exploded into protest.

'You know as well as I do, love—'

'I think what I said is true, all the same. You were at least half way to believing Ellen.'

'I wasn't.'

'Then it was an extremely anti-social action to release her on the public.'

'Jenny love, you know better than that. I was only doing my job, it was the jury who released her,' Antony explained earnestly. Jenny laughed, and began to explore the sides of the pudding dish for crispy bits of pudding. 'Seriously,' said her husband, grinning, 'I'd be very glad if I could believe her innocent, and still more glad if I thought I could prove it.'

'You've already—'

'By finding the real culprit, I mean, if he or she exists.'

'What's the next move then?' Roger asked.

'What I'd like to do would be to see Cox – Edward Gray's counsel – but he's been dead these ten years.'

'In his absence—?'

'I suppose to see the widow, Mrs Frances Wilcox.'

'Won't that be rather awkward?'

'It will. And that's an idea, Roger. You knew John Wilcox, why don't you come with me?'

'What good would that do?'

'It might oil the wheels a little.'

Roger hesitated only a moment. 'All right,' he said. 'When?'

'Now. Immediately, in fact, if you've finished. We could have coffee when we get back.'

'I might have known it.' Roger laid down his fork, and pushed his chair back a little from the table. 'If you'll excuse us, Jenny,' he said.

III

There was this added advantage to taking Roger with him, the Jensen was downstairs, so they didn't have to look for a taxi. Roger, who had a piratical look about him, and a habit of stirring up the company whenever he went into a room, had a sensitive streak as well, which rendered him extremely responsive to other people's moods. There was no need, therefore, for Antony to explain to him that he wanted to think, not talk, and the drive to the Wilcoxes' address in Bayswater was accomplished almost in silence.

They had taken a chance on finding Mrs Wilcox at home, rather than risk a rebuff on the telephone. It was Roy who let them in, and he had a puzzled look as he admitted that his mother was actually in the house. 'I've seen you somewhere before,' he said, directing a frowning look in Antony's direction.

'Indeed you have, in court. My name's Maitland,' said Antony. 'The one with the awkward questions,' he prompted, when Roy still looked confused.

'Ellen's counsel! You look quite different without your

124

wig. But I thought we'd seen the last of you,' said Roy gruffly.

'If we could just see your mother.'

'Well, I suppose ... but I can't see why.'

'It doesn't really matter, does it? This is Roger Farrell, a friend of your father's,' he added encouragingly. Roy's look from one of them to the other was still bewildered, but he backed away from the door, so that they could follow him into the hall.

'Just a minute.' Maitland's voice stopped him as he made for a door immediately on their right. 'Could you give me some idea of the lay-out here? Which is this room you're taking us to?'

'The morning-room. My mother uses it since ... well, we none of us fancy the drawing-room much now. That's at the other side of the hall, the door on the left.'

'Thank you. And the room where you and your sister were ... that night.'

'The dining-room is behind the morning-room ... that door there. But you had a plan in court, I saw it.'

'Nothing like seeing for yourself.'

'It's nothing to do with you now.'

'I hope your mother will be more kindly disposed towards me. Tell me, Roy, if somebody had come to the front door that night, and rung the bell, as we did, would you have heard it?'

'It chimes in the hall. There's just a chance we might not have heard it, if we were in the middle of a rally, but it's not very likely really. And anyway, Ellen had a key.'

'I meant, someone other than Ellen.'

'There wasn't time. Look, you've done enough harm already, do you really want to go on with this?'

'I'm afraid I do. If your mother will see us—'

'I'll ask her.' He shut the door of the morning-room firmly behind him, but was back in a moment saying, with a rather sulky look, 'She says to come in.'

Frances Wilcox was alone when they obeyed this rather grudging invitation, and a book lay face down on the sofa beside her. She was a little woman, with long dark hair taken up in a loose coil at the back of her head, and a permanently frowning look.

Roger took over the introductions, stressing his own liking for John Wilcox, his sympathy for her in her loss, and she began to look a little more relaxed. 'But I don't understand,' she said. 'Roy told me—'

'I'm sure he told you about Mr Maitland being here, because he had encountered him before.'

'Yes, he said ... in court. I don't understand,' she said again.

'We are sorry, we are both sorry to bring back memories that must be painful to you, but his visit concerns Miss Gray. If you will be kind enough to let him explain—'

'I don't want to hear anything about Ellen.'

'The jury found her innocent.'

'Yes, and I don't understand it.' She turned to Antony then. '*You* don't think she was guilty, but the case seemed so very clear.'

'If she really is innocent, don't you think she's had rather a hard time, and deserves some sympathy now? The thing is, there will always be people who suspect her – as you do, I think – until the real murderer is found.'

'And you think you can reopen the case again? On the assumption that she didn't kill my husband? I don't believe that, I'm afraid.'

'Won't you even admit the possibility that you may be wrong?'

'Roy says they heard the shot, and immediately afterwards found Ellen—' She faltered there, and Antony said, with quick sympathy,

'I'm sorry to distress you. But when you remember that you must also remember that Barbara said several minutes elapsed before they left the dining-room. If that is correct there was ample time for the murderer to leave and Ellen to arrive.'

'I don't like this, Mr Maitland, I don't like it at all.'

'Then let's agree to differ. I'd be infinitely obliged if you'd answer a few questions for me. Nothing to do with your husband's death at all ... or only indirectly.'

'Very well.' She glanced at Roger as she spoke. 'You'd better sit down, both of you. This room isn't as comfortable as ... but I like it better now.'

Antony took the chair at the other side of the fireplace from her – there was an electric fire there, with imitation coals – and Roger pulled his chair back a little, as though disassociating himself from the enquiry. When Antony started concentrating on anything, or anybody, it didn't do to interrupt. And Roger knew just how it would be; within a minute or two his friend would be as absorbed by his witness as ever he was in court. He'd have done well enough alone; but perhaps, after all, there had been some comfort in having a sympathetic companion in the first awkward moments of the encounter.

'First of all,' said Antony, 'a question the police must surely have asked you. Had your husband any enemies?'

'Of course he hadn't. He was – you said you knew him, Mr Farrell – a perfectly ordinary man.'

'Even quite ordinary men—'

'Well, there was nothing ... nobody. Everybody liked John.'

'It might not have been a question of liking. Something he knew ... something he had that somebody else wanted.'

'Unless you think I killed him, or one of the children, we were the only beneficiaries,' she said. The last word

127

seemed to have a wry taste in her mouth, and he hastened to reassure her.

'Of course I don't think anything of the kind. But there might have been someone—'

'There wasn't.'

'Something he knew, then, that was dangerous to some other person.'

'He'd have told me if there'd been anything like that.'

'If he'd had time.' But I wonder if he would have. Alison Clive had said, 'Frances is a worrier,' her husband's instinct might have been to avoid giving her cause. 'Was he quite his usual self the last day or two before he died?'

'Absolutely.'

'Are you sure of that, Mrs Wilcox?'

'Some days he was a little thoughtful. There was nothing out of the way about that. Oh, dear, I hope I'm doing the right thing, talking to you like this.'

'You're doing the kindest thing.'

'If you mean, to Ellen, I don't know that I want to be kind to her.'

You couldn't use the tactics of cross-examination here, or rely on the judge to intervene. Antony said, 'Please, Mrs Wilcox!' and Roger, watching, thought with amusement that the look he gave her would have melted a heart of stone, but the lady seemed strangely impervious. 'You're telling me – aren't you? – that he was a little thoughtful in the last days of his life.'

'He wasn't having a premonition, if that's what you mean.'

'I didn't mean that, as I think you know.'

'No, you meant that somebody else, not Ellen ... oh, this is all so useless, Mr Maitland.'

The only thing to do was to ignore that. 'He had something on his mind,' suggested Antony doggedly.

'There was nothing at home that could have bothered him, but he didn't always leave the office behind when he came home.'

'I see. About his friends now—'

'There are so many of them.'

'People he was intimate with, people he'd known for a long time.'

'They'd be less, rather than more likely to have hurt him.'

'Not necessarily. It's a poor argument, anyway, because you believe that Ellen killed him. And he'd known her a long time, hadn't he?' But Ellen, at eight years old, couldn't have fired the gun that killed her mother and Michael Foster.

'All her life. I've known her myself since she was four or five years old.'

'That was when you were married?'

'Yes.'

'Do you really think she could have changed so much, Mrs Wilcox? After all, you used to entrust your children to her care when they were younger.'

'She was a sly one, all right,' said Frances viciously.

Ignore that too. 'If you knew Ellen well all these years, it follows you know her guardians too.'

'Alison and Will. Yes, of course. Though I hardly knew them at all until Ellen went to live with them. They weren't part of the clique.'

He was immediately alert. 'The clique?' he repeated.

'There were three men John knew, whom he'd known since they were children together in the same suburb of Birmingham. Edward Gray was away at school with him; the others went to the local grammar school, as far as I remember, but they all remained close friends.'

'Until Edward Gray went to prison.'

'Yes, of course. You wanted the names of people who knew my husband well, Mr Maitland. Fred Tate and

Martin Roydon are certainly his oldest friends, as well as being very close to him.'

'You've known them yourself ever since you were married?'

'They were both in the Air Force, so I didn't get to know them well until after the war was over. John was away too, with the army, and it wasn't often they came on leave at the same time.'

'I see. But you think Gray would have been as closely in touch with them – all three – as his own service allowed?'

'Yes, I'm sure of it. I heard all about them from John, you know, even though I didn't see so much of them. At least – I'm misleading you – I must have seen Edward whenever he came home on leave, because Madeleine and I became good friends. Of course, being in the Far East, it was a long time since—'

'Then you can tell me how she took her husband's supposed death,' said Antony, when he was quite sure she didn't intend to finish the sentence.

'Badly. Then she pulled herself together, because of the child, I thought. But I never dreamed—' She broke off there, as far away from the Bayswater flat, Roger thought, as Antony himself was, back in wartime London.

'You never dreamed there was anything between her and Michael Foster. Is that what you meant, Mrs Wilcox?' Maitland prompted after a while.

'I ought to have known. I saw him often enough when I visited Madeleine.'

'What was he like?'

'An ordinary, dull young man. A bank clerk, I believe.'

'Not likely to inspire any very passionate attachment, you think?'

'I don't know. The most unlikely people fall in love with each other.'

'Yes, that's true,' he agreed, smiling faintly. 'But you

130

never saw anything to make you suspect—'

'I think now I was just being blind.'

'Don't say that.' He was smiling more openly now. 'I should be only too glad to be persuaded that Edward Gray had no cause for jealousy.'

'I can't think why you should concern yourself.'

'Because it might be the first step towards clearing Ellen's name. Come now, Mrs Wilcox, you were fond of her once. Surely you wouldn't mind—'

'Somebody killed my husband, Mr Maitland,' she told him sharply. 'And we know Ellen was here.'

'If Barbara was right—'

'I shouldn't count on it. Roy is by far the more observant of the two.'

'There is at least a chance that someone else came and went before Ellen arrived,' he insisted.

'Who then? One of John's close friends, you seem to be saying. I can tell you now I don't believe it.'

'Then let's go back to 1945. Do you remember the day Madeleine Gray and Michael Foster were killed?'

'Vividly.'

'The Grays had a flat on Putney Heath, is that right? And your husband was on his way to visit Madeleine when he met Edward in the street.'

'That's right. He came home so thrilled about it, because we had all thought Edward was dead, you know.'

'How did your husband come to be at home? Was he on leave?'

'No, he had already been demobilised.'

'Where did you live at that time?'

'Quite near the Grays. Another block of flats a little nearer to Roehampton.'

'Will you tell me exactly what your husband said when he got home that night?'

'After so long? I'm sure I can't remember.'

'Try.'

'Well, he went on foot, of course. He said as he got opposite the door of the Grays' block he met Edward coming in the opposite direction. They stood there talking for a few minutes, John was astonished, you can imagine that, and Edward asked him to go in with him but John thought it wouldn't be tactful to intrude just then. So he came straight home.'

'Did he notice whether Gray went immediately into his own block?'

'I think so. I'm not sure about that.'

'And how did he come to be so certain about the time?'

'It was a fad of John's to consult his watch very often. It would be second nature for him to look at it as they parted.'

'How long was he gone in all?'

'I'm not so accurate. About three-quarters of an hour, I should think.'

'And the walk would take—?'

'Five minutes. Less than that.'

'So his conversation with Gray was a prolonged one. Did he ever tell you what they had talked about?'

'How Edward came to be missing, I suppose, and why he didn't get back until so long after the war ended.'

'You "suppose", Mrs Wilcox. Don't you remember?'

'Not really.'

'Never mind.' The reassurance was unnecessary, Roger thought. If she was disappointing his friend, Frances Wilcox obviously couldn't care less. 'And you were at home when your husband left, and at home when he returned about three-quarters of an hour later?'

'Of course I was.' There was some sharpness in her tone again, and as if in answer to it Maitland came to his feet.

'I've kept you long enough from your book,' he said. 'But I can't tell you how grateful—'

'You needn't be.' She was on her feet too, perhaps

because she thought this might in some way speed the parting guests. 'I've talked to you against my better judgment, Mr Maitland. I don't think you should be encouraged in this crazy idea you've got.'

'Then it was all the more kind of you.'

'I hope you don't want to see Barbara, or Roy, because I won't allow—'

'Thank you, no.' There were some further civilities between them, in which Roger joined, but nothing that reduced in any way the feeling of tension that had grown up in the room. 'I don't think,' said Antony to Roger as they waited for the lift, 'that she could be any more glad to see us go than I am to be on our way.'

Roger didn't comment on that. 'Did you get what you wanted?' he asked.

'I shan't be really satisfied until someone hands me a motive for one, or both, of the murders,' Antony told him seriously. 'But, failing that, I don't think we did so badly. As far as opportunity goes, John Wilcox could certainly have murdered Madeleine and Michael Foster. So could Frances herself, for that matter.'

'If the two men were standing outside the door—'

'Ah, but there are two side entrances to that block. Ellen told me that, the first time I saw her.'

'Do you really think—?'

'Nothing, yet. I may know more – though I doubt it – when I've seen the other two members of this "clique" she talks about. I wonder who first applied that word to them.'

'Will you – would you like me to go along with you?'

Antony answered that with another question. 'Does that mean you're getting interested?'

'Of course I'm interested.'

'And don't join Mrs Wilcox in thinking me crazy?'

'If anybody ever had good reason to know that there's generally some kind of logic behind what you do—'

'This time I doubt it myself.'

'Well, I don't.'

'I'd be glad to have you with me,' said Antony, capitulating suddenly. Roger was surprised by this, but said nothing, and they arranged to see Frederick Tate, if possible, the following evening. But there was a surprise or two in store for Maitland before that.

IV

The first came in the shape of a telephone call, after Roger had left, but before they had started to prepare for bed. Antony was on his feet, however, and went across to answer it, and a voice that he didn't recognise said, without any more formal greeting, 'You're looking for trouble, you know.'

'I think,' said Antony, preparing to replace the receiver, 'you must have got the wrong number.'

'Oh, no, I'd know your voice anywhere, Mr Maitland. I was in court when you got that bitch, Ellen Gray, off a murder charge. Some of us don't think that was a good idea.'

'I really can't discuss—'

'You will, if you're wise.' It was a cultivated voice, a sleek, self-satisfied voice, and for some reason it grated on his nerves almost unbearably.

'If I'm going to listen to you, at least you can tell me who you are.'

'That doesn't concern you.'

'None of this conversation—'

'Don't be in too much of a hurry, Mr Maitland. You ought to thank me, really, for the warning, because you're meddling with something you don't understand. Don't take the matter any further, or you'll be sorry. I'm telling you this for your own good.'

'I don't understand, I'm afraid,' said Antony flatly.

'It should be clear enough. Leave Ellen Gray's affairs alone, she's no good, that girl. You'll only uncover something you won't like.'

The receiver was replaced then, very gently. Antony stood a moment before ringing off too, and then turned back to the room again. Jenny was still curled up in her favourite corner of the sofa, but her spine had stiffened and she was looking alert and anxious. 'Who was that?' she asked.

'Someone who doesn't like Ellen Gray. He didn't tell me his name. If anybody calls during the day, Jenny, don't listen. Just hang up right away.'

'Yes, but I don't like it, Antony. Did he threaten you?'

'Not very seriously.' He spoke lightly, and it wasn't only to reassure her; he was wondering now why for a moment the matter had seemed so important. 'Anybody in Ellen's position has enemies, love.'

'But you're not telling me properly, Antony. Did he know you'd opened the case again?'

'I think ... yes, I can only infer that he did,' he said slowly.

'That makes a difference, doesn't it? If somebody has been watching you—'

'Nobody has.' He spoke positively. 'It's just some crank, Jenny. Nothing to worry about.'

'That's easy to say. You really think nothing more will happen?'

'Who lives may learn. But yes, I do think so. Stop looking so anxious, Jenny, and come to bed.'

THURSDAY, 4th February

I

The second surprise came the following morning, when he turned back into chambers after seeing that amiable solicitor, Mr Bellerby, and one of his clients on their way. Mr Mallory was hovering, there was no other word for it, and that in itself was surprising because any message he wanted to give in person could easily have been delegated to one of the junior clerks. It turned out, however, that he wished to convey disapproval, and that was something that no-one else could do quite so well, or quite so subtly ... Sir Nicholas included. 'There is a Detective-Inspector Conway waiting to see you, Mr Maitland,' said Mr Mallory. 'I put him in the waiting-room.'

The information was startling enough to make Maitland impervious to the old man's displeasure. 'How long has he been there?' he asked, his tone unconsciously sharpening, so that Mallory added a frown to the other signs of his disapprobation.

'The best part of an hour,' he said. 'I gather his business with you must be of some urgency.'

The waiting-room was furnished as an office, and occasionally pressed into service as one. It was small and rather shabby, and – except for a bookcase full of out-of-date law books – held nothing to amuse or instruct the visitor. Not a place where one would willingly incarcerate one's worst enemy, nor – if one valued peace in our time – would you shut a man of Inspector Conway's temper up there for more than two minutes at once.

They obviously had an emergency on their hands, and Maitland went down the corridor quickly and flung open the door.

It was just as he had expected. Conway was bristling already, before they had exchanged one word. 'I'm sorry to have kept you waiting, Inspector,' said Antony mildly. 'If you'd phoned first Mallory could have told you I had a conference.'

'I wanted to see you,' said Conway coldly, 'at the first possible moment.'

'Well, this is it. Come along to my room, we shan't be disturbed there.' The detective followed him, positively radiating iciness, and Antony waved him to a chair as close as possible to the electric fire which was augmenting the central heating that chilly morning, in the hope of effecting a thaw. Conway, however, chose for himself the most penitential-looking of the three chairs which faced the desk, and hardly waited for Maitland to seat himself before launching himself into the more pressing of his grievances.

'I told your clerk the matter was urgent. He wouldn't interrupt you.'

'Very properly. That conference had been arranged for days, and however much I enjoy your company—'

'This is no time for banter, Mr Maitland. Let it pass that you were glad of the opportunity to keep me waiting.'

'I didn't even know you were here until just now,' Antony protested. He was inclined to be amused by the thoroughness with which the inspector had lost his temper, but he was curious as well, and on the whole that was the dominating emotion. So he resisted the temptation to throw fuel on the fire and said instead, in as equable a tone as he could manage, 'Let's not waste time now that we have got together. What can I do for you?'

'You can tell me what the devil you're playing at,

going to see Mrs Wilcox last night.' The mode of expression was a measure of Conway's loss of self-possession.

'Now, how did you know that?'

'She telephoned me this morning. The matter seemed to be preying on her mind.'

'I'm sorry about that, but if you spoke to her didn't she explain—?'

'Some nonsense about your re-opening the case.'

'Nonsense, Inspector! Let me remind you that Miss Gray was found Not Guilty.'

'In circumstances that even you—'

'Careful! You might find I resented any aspersions on my former client's character.'

There was a pause. 'Weren't you satisfied with getting the verdict?' Conway asked.

'At the time, I was. But when it was pointed out to me that Miss Gray's problems hadn't ended when she left the court—'

'Mr Maitland! Are you telling me that you believe in her innocence?'

'I'm telling you I think there is a case for further investigation.'

'That surely is a matter for the police.'

'It might be, if I thought for a moment you were going to undertake it. But the case is closed – isn't it? – as far as your records go.'

'Perhaps it is. But if you have any information—'

'So that's what's biting you,' said Antony incautiously. The temperature in the room immediately fell by several degrees. 'I haven't any information, Inspector, beyond what came out at the trial; and what little I gleaned from Mrs Wilcox last night ... and surely you must have talked to her yourself after her husband was killed.'

'I did, of course. But I don't think you quite realise, Mr Maitland, what I am trying to say to you. It is a serious matter to withhold information from the police.'

'I see. Would it make any difference if I assure you—'

'You would hardly be re-opening the matter without good cause.'

'Wouldn't I? I'm working on the assumption that Miss Gray is innocent, certainly—'

'Which you would hardly be doing in the absence of some hard fact.'

'No facts, Inspector. I could put up an argument, based on probabilities, which you wouldn't agree with for a moment.'

'I can see you've no intention of co-operating, Mr Maitland.'

'Don't worry. If my rooting about discloses anything startling, you'll be the first to know. I did have rather an interesting telephone call last night, but as it was anonymous it isn't much help to us.'

'You'd better tell me what was said,' said Conway grimly. And added, when Antony had done so, 'Are you trying to imply that the "real" murderer has been in touch with you.'

'Someone who doesn't like Miss Gray, that's all it purported to be,' said Antony, ignoring the sarcasm in the detective's tone. 'But I'm beginning to wonder—'

He wasn't allowed to finish. 'Mrs Wilcox says you also asked her questions about the murder of Madeleine Gray and Michael Foster,' said Conway, interrupting him.

Maitland's patience was wearing thin. 'Do you object to that too?' he asked.

'For the same reasons. Without some special knowledge you wouldn't be embarking on such an enquiry.'

'Look here, Inspector, we're getting nowhere. If you won't believe a word I say there's not much point in continuing this discussion.'

'What is your reason then . . . give me one good reason

why you should be asking questions about that old case?'
Conway demanded.

'That's an argument based on probabilities too. I
won't weary you with it.'

'I have to tell you, Mr Maitland, that I don't believe
you. Withholding information from the police—'

'Yes, you said that before. Tell me, Inspector, if Miss
Gray is really innocent—'

'I should be the first to want any injustice to be put
right,' said Conway stiffly.

'That's what I thought you'd say. So I can't see why
you object to what I'm trying to do.'

'Because it is an investigation that should properly be
conducted by the police.'

'Go ahead then, I'm not stopping you.'

'In the absence of any further information there is
nothing to investigate.'

'Nonsense, Inspector! There's always the chance that
something will turn up.'

'Not good enough, Mr Maitland.' Conway got to his
feet as he spoke. 'If you persist in this attitude there is
nothing further I can do, but I warn you—'

'Don't bother.' He began to move round the desk towards the door, but stopped when his hand was on the
knob. 'Tell me, Inspector, what did *you* think of the
outcome of Ellen Gray's trial?'

'I thought you had deceived yourself, and so deceived
the jury.'

Maitland smiled. 'Unkind!' he said. 'But I wonder,'
he added to himself a few minutes later after Inspector
Conway had gone, 'whether he – and Uncle Nick – could
possibly be right.'

140

The third surprise – it was more of a shock, really – came just after Roger arrived that evening, while Antony was finishing his second cup of coffee. The phone rang and Jenny answered it, and after a moment laid down the receiver and turned to her husband with a troubled look. 'It's someone for you, Antony,' she said. 'I don't know if it's the same person as last night, but he sounds awfully severe.'

Maitland got up reluctantly. It was bad enough having planned to go out that evening to see Fred Tate, without being prematurely disturbed by anonymous telephone calls. But when he got to the phone he found there was no anonymity about it, he recognised Inspector Conway's voice even before the detective announced himself. 'I hoped I'd convinced you this morning,' he said.

'Yes, I am quite aware that you are unwilling to co-operate with me. You needn't tell me *that* again,' said Conway waspishly. 'But something has happened today which perhaps may change your mind. Mrs Wilcox has been found dead in her flat in Bayswater.'

Antony said, 'What!' rather too loudly for the comfort of the person at the other end of the line, and Conway's voice sounded remote as well as austere when he repeated his statement. 'When was she found? How did she die?' Maitland demanded.

'She was found at about half past four by her daughter, when the girl returned from the Art School which she attends.' It didn't need underlining that Conway disapproved of Art Schools. 'Their doctor has declined to issue a death certificate.'

'Well, was it anything obvious? Another shooting perhaps?'

'Nothing obvious, Mr Maitland. An autopsy is being performed.'

'Poison? If that doesn't put the cat among the pigeons!' said Antony, and was immediately reproved.

'I haven't said so. That I have told you so much is due only to the hope that perhaps this might change your mind.'

'Has it changed yours, Inspector? Are you going to re-open the matter of John Wilcox's death?'

'If circumstances warrant it.'

'Damn it, there must be some connection. Unless—'

'The circumstances are such as to make suicide unlikely.'

'In that case—'

'I'm not arguing about the connection, Mr Maitland. It may be closer than you will wish to acknowledge.'

'You're trying to tell me you think Ellen Gray—?'

'The matter is under investigation. It would be improper for me to say more.' Conway was keeping his temper this evening. It might be he thought that he had Maitland at a disadvantage. 'But I do urge you, if you have anything to tell me—'

'Nothing, Inspector. Nothing at all. I told you that, if you remember.'

'At least, from now on, perhaps you will leave matters where they belong, in the hands of the police,' said Conway, with a sudden increase in asperity.

'There's no harm in hoping,' said Antony; and added, 'Good night,' and replaced the receiver gently. When he turned round he realised that neither Jenny nor Roger was making any pretence of inattention, but had been listening unashamedly.

'Was that Inspector Conway again?' asked Jenny. And, 'Who's been poisoned?' demanded Roger, almost in the same moment.

'It was indeed Inspector Conway, full of goodwill,' said

Antony. He smiled as he came back to the hearth again, but his eyes had a worried look. 'Frances Wilcox is dead, Roger. As far as I could tell from what Conway didn't say, poison is suspected.'

'But only last night—' said Roger. Antony ignored that.

'Conway's attitude isn't very clear. On the one hand he was hinting at murder. On the other he seems to blame what Uncle Nick always calls my meddling for her death.'

'Oh, that's nonsense!' said Jenny quickly.

'If she was really upset at being reminded of her husband's death—'

'She wasn't in a suicidal frame of mind,' said Roger positively. 'And if she had been she'd hardly have waited until today.'

'I don't think that follows. I thought when I saw her that she had something on her mind.'

'Not suicide.'

'No, I don't think so. Conway was also hinting that Ellen Gray might have done this too, making a clean sweep of the family, I suppose. I'd better talk to Geoffrey, don't you think?'

But when he tried to phone the solicitor a few minutes later, there was no reply from his home.

'In that case,' said Antony, coming away from the phone, and this time more reluctantly, 'we'd better change our minds, Roger, and I'll go and see Ellen instead.'

'Do you think that's a good idea?'

'Yes, because somebody should be there to prevent her from saying all the wrong things when Conway gets round to interviewing her.'

'Suppose Conway's right.'

'He may be.' He paused there, looking from one to the other of his companions. 'Doesn't what's happened today make you think it's all the more likely that she's altogether innocent?'

'We've both of us been taking your word for that,' Jenny reminded him.

'In spite of my own doubts?'

'In which we don't altogether believe,' Roger pointed out.

'Simple faith? I suppose I should say that's very gratifying, but I think on the whole I'd rather you took my word for them. However, today ... why the hell should Ellen have murdered Mrs Wilcox, anyway?'

'Why should anybody?'

'That's true, there's no obvious motive. Should I phone Doctor Clive to warn him? No, I think I'll just get over there right away.'

'I'll drive you,' Roger offered.

'Thanks, but it would mean waiting about. I think this evening I'd do better on my own.'

'That's all right. I'll have a pint at the King's Head while I'm waiting for you, and you can join me there when you get through.'

'In that case—' He left it there, but Roger understood him and came to his feet. 'I don't suppose I'll be late, Jenny love, but don't wait up for me.'

III

Afterwards he felt it was no more than he should have expected, that he should encounter Detective-Inspector Conway on the doorstep of the Clives' house in Roehampton Lane. Roger had dropped him at the end of the short drive, and driven off without seeing the other car that was parked near the front door. Antony came up the steps and found that Conway had already rung the bell, and sustained a look of furious disapprobation with equanimity. The detective was accompanied by a colleague, Detective-Sergeant Mayhew, whom also Antony already knew. The Sergeant was younger and heavier than his superior, had a shock of dark hair, a stolid look, and a nice sense of humour which was usually kept strictly under control. He said nothing now beyond, 'Good evening, Mr Maitland,' but Antony immediately felt — perhaps it was a dangerous feeling — that here he had found a friend.

Conway did not confine himself to 'Good evening,' did not even utter the greeting, but said, 'I might have known!' in an over-wrought way.

Antony smiled at him. 'Yes, I think in all the circumstances you should have guessed. I shouldn't be here, of course, if Mr Horton had been at home.'

If the Inspector was listening he gave no sign. 'Three times in one day!' he said. 'Three times in one day!'

'If you can count a telephone conversation. And let me point out that it was all your doing; just as it's your doing, in a way, that I'm here now.'

At this point the door was opened by Ellen Gray, who looked at Inspector Conway as though he had been a ghost, and then from him to Antony in plain bewilderment. 'I'm afraid, Miss Gray,' said Conway briskly, 'we have a few questions to put to you.'

'But you can't ... it's all over ... and what are *you* doing with the police?' she added, with a piercing look in Antony's direction. His answer was as bracing as he could make it.

'Protecting your interests,' he said, 'as Mr Horton wasn't to be found. And, of course, it isn't about John Wilcox's death that Inspector Conway wants to talk to you. Something else has happened.'

'If you will allow me, Mr Maitland,' Conway broke in. 'Perhaps we may come inside, Miss Gray, this isn't the sort of conversation that should be held on the doorstep.

And then you can decide whether you want Mr Maitland to be present during the interrogation.'

Ellen had been pale before, now she looked ready to faint. Maitland said, as she backed away and they crowded into the hallway, 'If Miss Gray decides to answer your questions, it will only be after you have told her exactly why you wish to ask them.'

'Very well,' Conway snapped, without removing his eyes from Ellen's face. 'Perhaps ... is Doctor Clive in, Miss Gray? He ought to hear what I have to say.'

'He's ... in the drawing-room. My aunt went to bed, she isn't feeling well,' said Ellen jerkily. Sergeant Mayhew closed the front door, took a step further into the hall, and coughed.

'If you will show us the way, Miss Gray,' he said.

'I'm surprised you don't remember,' said Ellen, with the first flash of spirit she had shown. But she opened the door and said as she went in, fairly steadily, 'Uncle Will, there are the two men from the police who were here before. Inspector Conway, and ... and—'

'Detective-Sergeant Mayhew,' Maitland supplied. 'Inspector Conway has sometning to tell you both, Doctor, but first I think Miss Gray should sit down.'

Doctor Clive had got to his feet and retreated a pace or two, rather as if he were prepared to sell his life dearly. He said now, 'Of course, of course. Whatever is the matter, my dear?' and took Ellen's hands and guided her to the chair he had been occupying. 'You'd better sit down, all of you,' he said over his shoulder, but both the detectives ignored the offer, and Antony moved across the room until he could stand at Ellen's elbow. Unexpectedly, she looked up at him with naked appeal in her eyes, and said in a low voice,

'You will stay, won't you?'

'That's what I'm here for,' he told her, and hoped his smile conveyed some reassurance. 'Now you must listen to what Inspector Conway has to say.'

The doctor had sat down again at the opposite side of the hearth. He still looked bewildered, which perhaps wasn't surprising, but he said, 'Yes, yes, somebody should explain,' quite testily.

'Very well,' said Conway again, not liking the position into which he had been manoeuvred. 'I am sorry to have to inform you that Mrs John Wilcox is dead.'

'Frances?' said the doctor incredulously. 'But only last night—'

'She was here, doctor?' Conway pounced as Doctor Clive broke off.

'No, she telephoned me. After you left her, Mr Maitland. She seemed disturbed, but there was nothing to indicate—'

'You're assuming she took her own life,' Conway interrupted him.

'Her health was good, so far as I know. And in the tragic circumstances—'

He seemed fated not to complete a sentence. 'I'd better make it clear once and for all,' Conway said, with a look of loathing in Maitland's direction. 'Poison is suspected. A specific poison, morphine, though that is yet to be confirmed. The flat has been searched, and there is no indication at all that she had such a thing in her possession. Which seems to suggest that somebody else took the poison there and administered it.'

'When did she die?' Antony interposed, judging from William Clive's expression that he was for the moment speechless. 'You want something from us, Inspector,' he added softly. 'You'll only get it if you make a fair return.'

'If you must know, Mr Maitland, not much more than half an hour before her daughter found her.'

'Then when did she take the poison?'

'As we don't yet know—'

147

'Doctor?'

'Assuming it was morphine in a fatal dose,' said William Clive, shaken, but doing his best. 'Anything from half an hour to six hours previously. That's generalising, you know, it's very tricky stuff and the effect on different people differs enormously. Also the quantity taken would make a difference, of course.'

'I see.' He put out a hand and touched Ellen's shoulder, so that she looked up at him. 'Would you like to answer Inspector Conway's questions now?' he asked. 'Or would you rather wait until Mr Horton is available? And you're quite within your rights – I expect you know that – not to say anything at all.'

'I've nothing to hide, but I can't promise to be able to tell the Inspector anything.' He was startled, and a little uneasy, at the change in her. This was a girl who might not have known the meaning of the word 'apathy'. She looked wary, but every inch a fighter.

'You'd like me to be present? I'm only here as a friend, you know.'

'I thought—'

'On the principle that if I were a strong swimmer I wouldn't watch another man drown because I didn't happen to be on life guard duty.'

Ellen smiled at him then. So far as he could remember it was the first time he had seen her smile, and he found himself regretting that the opportunity came so rarely. 'I don't understand at all,' she said. 'But I should like you to stay, and Uncle William too.'

The doctor muttered something that sounded like, 'Of course, of course.' Ellen Gray turned back to face the inspector, and folded her hands composedly in her lap.

'Well?' she said.

'If Mr Maitland has quite finished—' said Conway, at his most sarcastic. Antony caught Mayhew's eye, and suppressed a smile when the sergeant gave another of his warning coughs and said, in his deep voice,

'I think you'll find he'll let you get on with it now, sir.'

Conway flashed him an injured look; perhaps he expected his sergeants to be seen and not heard. 'Very well then,' he said, a trifle portentously, 'we will come at once to the heart of the matter. Will you give me an account of your movements today, Miss Gray?'

'She has been at work, of course, Stephen Langland can speak to that,' said William Clive before his niece could speak.

'I think we must let Miss Gray answer for herself, doctor.'

'Well, no, I wasn't there all day,' said Ellen unwillingly. Antony thought it was more that she hesitated to contradict her uncle than that she dreaded the effect of the admission. 'I left my job at noon, and came home to lunch as usual. Afterwards I went out again ... walking.'

'Can anyone substantiate that?'

'That I went on the heath? No, I didn't meet anyone I know.'

'Then I must ask you, Miss Gray, when was the last time you saw Mrs Wilcox?'

'Before ... before John was killed.'

'Were you in Bayswater today?'

'No, I told you. I was in Putney at work all the morning, and on Putney Heath this afternoon.'

'When you say you left your job—?'

'I mean just that. I left it for good.'

'Why was that?'

'I don't think that concerns you, Inspector.'

'If you won't be frank with me, Miss Gray—'

'Not relevant,' said Maitland with finality. 'And now let me ask a question. Admitting that Frances Wilcox was murdered – about which you seem to be in some doubt

149

– why does that bring you hotfoot to Roehampton to see Miss Gray?'

'Because fingerprints which I strongly suspect to be hers were found in the room where Mrs Wilcox died.'

'You ... strongly suspect?' Then, when he got nothing from Conway but an inimical look, he went on, 'Your fingerprints chap is an expert, of course. He remembered the characteristics. Is that right?'

'Quite right. So I think Miss Gray has some explaining to do,' said Conway, who obviously felt he was in the position of having turned the tables.

'What room—?'

'The drawing-room.'

'Nobody denies that Miss Gray has been there many times.'

'If you will have it in words of one syllable, Mr Maitland, the room must have been thoroughly cleaned after John Wilcox's death, after the fingerprint men were through with it. Therefore—'

'I think any explanations from Miss Gray must wait until you are certain of your facts, Inspector.'

'Is that your wish, Miss Gray?'

'They ... couldn't be there,' said Ellen, shaking her head in a bewildered way. And then, more confidently, 'In any case, I have no explanation to offer.'

'So you see—' said Maitland, who wasn't altogether pleased by this exchange, though he realised he had no official standing on which to base a protest.

'I see you are bent on circumventing me at every turn,' said Conway waspishly. 'And if you think I have quite finished, think again. There is also the question of the poison used.'

'Morphine,' said Antony, drawing out the word thoughtfully. 'Though you seem in some doubt about that too.'

'Not much doubt. And I may tell you to begin with

that Mrs Wilcox's doctor never prescribed anything of the kind for her, or for any member of the family.'

'Yes, I see. You are about to remind us—' He broke off as Mayhew gave his warning cough.

'It has its medicinal uses. But you can't exactly buy it over the counter like a packet of tea,' said the sergeant.

Maitland said nothing. 'So you see,' said Conway, seemingly pleased this time with his subordinate's interruption, 'whoever administered it had to get hold of it somehow. And what with Miss Gray living in a doctor's household—'

'Oh, no, no, no!' William Clive came to life suddenly. 'There can be no question of that. My records will show that everything is in order.'

'I'm sure I hope so, doctor,' said Conway insincerely. 'Nevertheless, I am going to ask you to let me seal the cupboard in which your drugs are kept, and to allow access to your records tomorrow, so that a check may be made.'

'There can be no objection to that. I am only too eager to allow you to see that you are mistaken.'

'I wonder if Miss Gray is quite so confident.' Ellen made no reply, but merely jutted her chin at him. 'Well, if you will show me the way, doctor, I shan't bother you any further this evening. Good-night to you, Miss Gray. Good-night, Mr Maitland.' The two detectives followed Doctor Clive out of the room.

As soon as the door closed behind them Ellen was on her feet. 'That man!' she said. 'I thought he was going to arrest me.'

'Not without further evidence.'

'You mean, if Uncle Will has made any sort of mistake in his records—'

'Do you really think that's likely? He strikes me as being a careful sort of man.'

'He is, of course. Mr Maitland, is it any good my telling you that I had nothing to do with this, any more than I had to do with John's death?'

'In the circumstances, I find the assurance comforting.' She looked at him doubtfully. 'Will you tell me, Miss Gray, why you left your job so suddenly?'

'I thought ... I don't know ... it didn't seem fair to Stephen. But now, for some reason, things seem different. Do you think I should fight?'

For the moment he was supremely confident. 'Of course you should!' he told her. Ellen put out her hand unexpectedly and touched his sleeve.

'I think you're starting to believe in me,' she said.

He considered that for a moment, and then laughed. 'My uncle would tell you I've believed in you all along,' he said.

'Well, that's a change. But you're going to help me, Mr Maitland. I feel much better about things, knowing that.'

'I'm going to help you *if I can*, Miss Gray. You mustn't expect too much, you know.'

'Nothing less than the moon and the stars,' said Ellen ebulliently. 'And I think ... do you know, Mr Maitland, I think I'll go back to work tomorrow.'

IV

Nothing could have been better calculated to facilitate his descent into the depths of gloom. 'I tried to explain the difficulties to her,' he protested to Roger when they were in the car again and driving up Roehampton Lane, 'but for some reason she's got it fixed in her head that I'm going to put everything right. And I'm not even sure, though I was for a moment ... she may have been trying to plant the idea in my head that her uncle might have made a mistake in his records.'

'I shouldn't worry about that until it gets up and bites you,' said Roger. 'Trust your instinct, it's been right before.'

'But not always, as Uncle Nick would tell you.'

'In any case, it's surely better to have a cheerful client than an apathetic one.' Roger was determined to look on the bright side.

'She's not my client, at this stage of the game,' Antony corrected him automatically. 'And I must say I'd rather almost anybody had the case rather than Conway. Which reminds me, I haven't seen Uncle Nick since Conway came to chambers this morning. He won't be pleased with me, I'm afraid.'

'I don't quite see—'

'He says it's my own fault that the police are invariably out for blood when I appear on the horizon. And he may be right, Roger, he may be right.'

V

The parking space in front of Number Five, Kempenfeldt Square, was occupied by a blue Hillman when they arrived there; to Roger's annoyance, because he had come to regard the space as peculiarly his own. They found an opening opposite Number Thirteen, and were walking back when the doors of the usurping car shot open suddenly, and two men got out.

The nearer of the two was short and powerfully built, and – except for his height – reminded Antony vaguely of Sergeant Mayhew. His companion, coming round the car to his side, was revealed as being of medium height and slender build, with something almost foppish about his dress. They stood quite still, waiting for Antony and Roger to come up with them, and effectively blocking the way to the steps in front of Number Five. There was no doubt in Maitland's mind, even before either of them spoke, that their intent was hostile. His injured shoulder made him ineffective as a combatant, but he had great faith in Roger if it came to a scrap, and he still knew a trick or two that might be used to good effect.

It seemed, however, that the present intent of the two men was merely conversational. When Roger said, 'You're in our way, you know,' neither of them made any reply, though the foppish man sniggered.

The other said, looking from one of them to the other, 'Which of you two is Maitland?'

Antony was standing very still. Only Roger, who knew him well, could have supposed that this might be the prelude to sudden action. He said, mildly, 'Hadn't you better introduce yourselves first?' and the taller of the two men laughed again.

'Well, it makes no odds,' he said. 'One of you is, because we watched you drive off and there's no mistaking that car.'

'Well?'

'We've got a message for you, like,' said the shorter man. 'The boss was sorry he couldn't come himself.'

'Indeed? Now you do interest me,' said Antony politely.

'He warned you last night, and we're warning you again now. Lay off Ellen Gray's affairs.'

'And if I don't?'

'You'd better!' The two men stepped aside then, as if the movement had been rehearsed, leaving the way clear to the steps. 'That's all,' said the one who seemed to have elected himself spokesman.

Antony and Roger exchanged a glance, and then Antony led the way up the steps. He had an idea that Roger was just faintly disappointed at such a tame outcome to the proceedings, but for himself his only desire was for five minutes' quiet to think things over. When he had got his key in the lock he glanced back to see the two men still standing looking up at them, but he made no comment and led the way into the hall. 'What do you make of that?' asked Roger, as soon as the door was closed.

'I'm beginning to get ideas,' said Antony. The study door was safely shut, though a line of light beneath it showed that Sir Nicholas had not yet retired. 'I mean, unless Ellen Gray's ill-wishers have formed a sort of club—'

'I agree that isn't likely. So what follows?'

'Give me time, Roger.' He produced a crumpled envelope and a stub of pencil from his pocket and scribbled something down. 'The number of the car,' he said. 'Before I forget.'

'Not very bright of them to leave it in front of the house, was it?'

'Not bright at all, but I expect they wanted to keep warm. Let's hope it proves useful.'

'Are you going to tell Conway?'

'I haven't much alternative if I want to find out who owns the car.'

'I thought perhaps Chief Inspector Sykes—'

'It would put him in an awkward position, seeming to interfere in another man's case. No, it will have to be Conway.'

'Yes, of course.' They began to go up the stairs, Antony again in the lead. 'No need to mention that little encounter to Jenny, I suppose,' said Roger, as they neared the first landing.

'Heaven forbid,' said Antony piously.

Roger stayed with them for about twenty minutes longer, before he left to collect Meg from the theatre.

When he went the Hillman car was gone from the parking space outside Number Five.

There was no telephone call, or any other disturbance, that night.

FRIDAY, 5th February

I

Right or wrong, Sir Nicholas had every intention of having his say, and came upstairs while they were still at breakfast the next morning. Jenny offered him coffee, which he refused; but she fetched another cup and after a while he drank what she provided, but absent-mindedly. 'It's really nothing I can do anything about,' said Antony patiently when the older man's quiet tirade had finished. 'Conway's contention is that I must know something the police don't, and that I ought to tell them. I only wish it were true.'

'All the same, from his point of view it is not un-reasonable,' Sir Nicholas mused. Adding, in an acid tone a moment later, 'He can hardly be expected to appreciate the very slender grounds you require for undertaking an investigation of this kind.'

'But I explained to you on Tuesday, Uncle Nick—'

'Some nonsense about probabilities. You cannot ex-pect the police to appreciate anything so tenuous.'

'I don't expect anything from Conway except trouble. If it was in the paper this morning I didn't see it ... Frances Wilcox is dead too. The police suspect murder.'

'Frances? The daughter?'

'No, John Wilcox's widow. I went to see Ellen Gray last night, and Conway was there.'

Sir Nicholas was in no mood for smiling, but at this he came close to it. 'I can appreciate his sentiments,' he said. 'I suppose you insisted on interfering.'

'In Geoffrey's absence ... which reminds me, I must phone Geoffrey this morning.'

'Am I to understand that the police suspect Ellen Gray of this killing too?'

'They found some fingerprints. And as the woman apparently died of morphine poisoning—'

'They think it would be a tidy solution if the suspect came from a doctor's household. I can sympathise with that too. How likely do you think it is to be the truth?'

That was an awkward question. Last night ... but the morning had brought, not counsel (except in the shape of his uncle) but some very agonising doubts. 'I'd rather you didn't ask that, Uncle Nick,' he said frankly. And then, gloomily, 'Ellen Gray has quite made up her mind that I'm about to work a miracle.'

'If you led her to think anything of the kind—'

Jenny was moved to protest. 'Of course he didn't, Uncle Nick. But he can't help it if people trust him.'

'The more fool they,' said Sir Nicholas disagreeably. 'But you didn't answer my question, Antony.'

'I don't see Doctor Clive being careless with the key to his poison cupboard,' said Antony. His uncle looked at him for what seemed like a long minute.

'Hmm,' he said at last. 'I suppose that is an answer, of a sort.' He drank the last of his coffee, and came to his feet. 'I must be off,' he said. 'Are you coming, Antony?'

'I may as well.' Maitland got up too, but more reluctantly. 'If you're taking a cab, Uncle Nick, I'll be glad of a lift. Things seem to be piling up rather at the moment.'

That was an incautious remark. 'If you would keep your mind on your work—' Sir Nicholas was saying as they went out of the room. Jenny listened, smiling to herself, until the closing door cut off his voice. Then she shook the coffee pot enquiringly and, reassured by what she heard, settled herself down to have another cup.

When Antony had a quiet moment, at about the time his afternoon tea arrived, he telephoned Scotland Yard and asked for Detective-Inspector Conway. To his surprise, he got through without delay; perhaps the detective was having a quiet moment too. 'Well, Mr Maitland?' said Conway's voice coldly in his ear.

No use starting out by being apologetic. 'Something's happened that I think you ought to hear,' said Antony abruptly. And went on to tell the inspector of the encounter the evening before, to give him the number of the blue Hillman, and to describe the two men as well as he could.

Conway listened without comment, and was silent for a moment after he had finished, so that Antony said, 'Hallo?' anxiously, in case they had been cut off. 'I'm still here, Mr Maitland,' said the detective then. 'I'm just wondering what you expect to gain by telling me this extraordinary story.'

'Then you agree it's extraordinary. That's what I thought too. I thought you might find out for me who owns the car, and if you know anything about him.'

'Are you under the impression that there is something you can charge him with?'

'Of course I'm not! It might help me with the puzzle I've set myself, that's all.'

'I'm not at all sure that I want to encourage you. If this story is true—'

'It's t-true,' said Antony, who didn't relish, any more than the next man, being called a liar. 'C-come now,' he added, making a great effort to control his annoyance, 'won't you at least write down the number of the car?'

'I have already done so, Mr Maitland.'

'Then I'll look forward to hearing from you.'

'You may do so, of course, but I shouldn't count on it,' said Conway, and replaced the receiver without any words of farewell.

III

That evening the projected visit to Frederick Tate actually took place, and true to his promise Antony took Roger along with him. He wasn't quite sure what instinct told him it would be as well to have a witness to what was said, he only knew it was a strong one. And Roger had what might be considered an uncharacteristic ability to efface himself when he wished – which in the ordinary way wasn't often – that made him an ideal companion at a time like this.

So they made their way to Wood Green where the Tates had a home on land that seemed to have been only recently developed, an area of what were probably advertised as 'executive homes'. This time Antony had phoned in advance, and they were greeted on the doorstep before they had time to ring the bell. 'That's a grand car,' said Fred Tate after they had introduced themselves, eyeing the sleek lines of the Jensen a trifle enviously. 'Is it yours, Mr Maitland?'

'My – er – my colleague's,' said Antony, hesitating over even this small deception in face of Tate's obvious friendliness.

'Well, come in, come in. I've been looking forward to talking to you,' said Tate with obvious sincerity. 'It isn't every day—' He broke off there, as if he had forgotten what he was going to say, but covered any possible embarrassment with a boisterous laugh.

He led them to a room on the right of the hall, a room that was large and well furnished, but not very tidy, in spite of the fact that every stick of furniture looked brand new. 'Mr Maitland and Mr Farrell, Matty. My wife, gentlemen,' said Tate exuberantly. And began to manhandle chairs into what he seemed to consider a more favourable position.

Mathilda Tate smiled her acknowledgement of the introduction, but otherwise took no notice of his gyrations. She was a woman of medium height, with brown hair that curled closely over her head, and Alison Clive's description of her as 'placid' seemed to Antony extremely apt. And perhaps, too, you needed a certain calmness of disposition to survive at all in that fervid atmosphere. When her husband had arranged matters to his satisfaction she waved a hand in an encouraging way and the two visitors sat down, though Antony at least half expected the chair to be whirled away from under him in some renewed spurt of energy on the part of their host. Nothing untoward happened, however, and after a moment Tate went back to his own place beside the hearth. 'I've said I'm pleased to see you, Mr Maitland,' he said, 'since you say I can help you. But I'm damned if I know what you're doing here.'

'Have you heard what happened yesterday?'

'Frances Wilcox?' He was immediately sober. 'Yes, poor girl. That was a terrible thing.'

'Terrible,' echoed Mathilda. She had a rather deep, pleasant voice, and Roger looked at her with interest. But Maitland's attention was already fixed on Fred Tate.

And Fred, it appeared, had some tenacity of purpose, for he said now, insistently, 'But that doesn't explain—'

Antony countered with a question. 'You gave character evidence on Ellen Gray's behalf, Mr Tate. How did you feel about that?'

'I told no more than the truth.'

'Yes, of course, I'm sure of that. But did you feel you were helping an innocent girl, or putting the best face on it for someone who had been your friend but was now a murderer?'

Fred laughed again, for no very obvious reason, and it was his wife who replied first, saying quietly, 'We have always had a great affection for Ellen, Mr Maitland.'

Antony turned to her. 'But that doesn't answer my question, Mrs Tate. Or does it?' he added, smiling at her.

'I think perhaps it does.'

'I see. If your husband feels the same way—'

'I do, I do,' said Fred, rather hurriedly.

'—that makes things a little awkward. Because it's on Miss Gray's behalf that I'm here.'

'You think she's innocent.'

Again he came back with a question. 'Don't you agree that John and Frances Wilcox's deaths must be connected?'

'Unless she—'

'The police are acting on the assumption that it is murder. My latest information' – culled late that afternoon from Geoffrey Horton – 'is that morphine poisoning has been confirmed.'

'Well then, I suppose—' Tate seemed incapable of completing a sentence.

'I'll go further. I'll say it's too much of a coincidence if the crime of which Ellen's father was accused is unconnected with the other two.'

'Oh, come now!' said Fred. Mathilda held up a hand as though forbidding him to say anything more.

'Wait a bit, Fred,' she commanded. 'There may be something in what Mr Maitland says. And certainly Ellen didn't shoot her mother and Michael.'

'I'm damned if I know why she should kill Frances

either,' said Fred thoughtfully. 'But if she didn't, who did?'

'That's what I'd like to find out. You were a close friend of the Grays up to the time of Edward's arrest, Mr Tate. That's why I come to you.'

'You can't hope to find out anything at this date—'

'I don't really hope, to tell you the truth, but it seems I've got to try. Ellen's position was intolerable, even before Mrs Wilcox's death; which is grossly unfair, if she's innocent.'

'I wonder how sure you are about that,' said Fred shrewdly. Again Mathilda held up a hand as though to quiet him.

'I think you ought to do what you can to help Mr Maitland,' she said. 'And if Ellen is innocent, I for one shall be glad to hear it.'

'Well, so shall I, of course,' Fred protested. 'What sort of help do you need?'

'That you'll answer a few questions. If you remember that I'm groping in the dark, as it were ... I mean, I don't want to have to explain "Why?" all the time. If you're confused by the situation, so am I.'

'All right.' Oddly enough, that sounded rather like a threat. 'We'll do what we can,' he went on, in a lower key. 'Though as far as Matty's concerned, of course, she never knew Edward or Madeleine.'

'Do you remember the night Edward Gray came home?'

'Of course I do. I was on leave, staying at an hotel in town. I didn't hear what had happened until the following day, of course.'

'Mrs Wilcox told us that her husband had already been demobbed. What about Mr Roydon? He was Air Force too, wasn't he? Was he also on leave by any chance?'

Fred Tate gave him rather a sharp look at that, but he made no open comment. 'He wasn't on leave, but he
163

was stationed at Uxbridge,' he said. 'In the filter room. I saw a good deal of him, one way and another, while I was at home.'

'Did you see him that night?'

'No. I stayed in for him too, but he wasn't able to get away. Funny how clearly I remember it after all these years.'

'It seems quite reasonable to me,' Antony told him. 'What happened would impress it on your mind, don't you think?'

Fred Tate gave him an amused look, but his comment was an indirect one. 'No alibis for either of us,' he said. 'And now I come to think of it, no alibi for John either, in fact the opposite, if there is such a thing.'

'That's a horrible thing to say, Fred,' said Matty.

'Not really because, as Mr Maitland is about to point out to us, John didn't shoot himself, and he certainly didn't poison Frances. And as we seem to be working on the theory—'

'Then you're saying that either you or Martin ... that's a horrible thing to say,' she said again.

'I'm not saying that at all, but I think Mr Maitland may be getting ready to. Isn't that so?' he asked. There seemed to be no malice in his tone, only curiosity.

'I told you I was groping in the dark,' said Antony.

'So you did. Well, after establishing that we were all within striking distance of Putney on the night in question ... what now?'

'You knew Madeleine Gray. I suppose you knew Michael Foster too.'

'Not well, but I got the impression he was a frequent visitor.'

'Did you also suspect that there was anything between them?'

'I didn't suspect it. I was surprised when I heard. But afterwards ... it seemed so obvious.'

164

'I see. What was Foster like?'

'Very quiet. Matty would say that was only because no-one gets much chance to talk when I'm about. But seriously, I thought he probably had hidden depths.'

'Why?'

'I thought that question was *verboten*.'

'Only to you.'

'Well, I suppose because Madeleine seemed to enjoy his company, and she wasn't all that easily pleased.'

'Do you remember the last time you saw her?'

'Very well. It was the Sunday before she was killed.'

'Was that at the Putney flat?'

'Yes.'

'And was Foster there?'

'No, for a wonder. But Martin was.'

'Can you remember ... was everything just as usual? Did her manner seem different in any way?'

'If it had I'd have remembered in view of what happened so shortly afterwards. She'd been quiet ever since Edward went missing, of course.'

'But that evening—'

'Oh, for heaven's sake, man, she didn't foresee her own death!'

'That wasn't what I meant. If she had something on her mind—'

Again Tate interrupted him. 'Well, in the light of what happened I wondered if she'd been trying to get up courage to tell us about Michael. It would have come as a bit of a shock, I can tell you that, coming so soon after.'

'That's on the theory that Edward killed them. But for the moment we're giving him the benefit of the doubt ... remember?'

'So we are,' said Fred blandly.

'You seem to be saying there *was* something different about Madeleine.'

'It might have been any one of a thousand things.'

This time Fred sounded a little impatient. 'Ellen might not have been well ... she may have felt a bit off colour herself ... anything!'

'I'm sorry to press the matter, but it really is important. Did she say anything that might give us a clue?'

'Nothing at all.'

Reluctantly, Antony left the subject. 'When did you last see Edward Gray?' he asked.

'The leave before he went missing. Some time before, that's something I don't remember exactly.'

'Not at his trial?'

'I was back on duty, such as it was with the war not long over. John told me about it, of course.'

'Did John Wilcox ever tell you what he and Edward talked about when they met so unexpectedly that night?'

'Of course he did. Edward was telling him where he'd been, what had happened to him. But nobody ever did explain how it came about that Madeleine hadn't been advised that he was on his way home.'

'That doesn't matter so much. But where he'd been, and all the rest of it, that interests me.'

'I can only give it to you at second hand,' Fred warned him.

'Which is the best anybody can do now.'

'All right then. He was captured by the Japanese, put to work on the Thailand railway, and eventually escaped into the jungle. After that it was a matter of keeping walking – a very tricky business I should say – until he finally made contact with some unit or other of the Allied Forces. That was the first he'd known of the war being over.' Tate gave Antony another of his shrewd looks. 'Not what you wanted to hear,' he said.

'He'd been through a good deal. He'd be on edge when he got back, and somebody said he had a hair-trigger temper.'

'I wouldn't have put it quite so strongly. But as you're saying – I think – he'd have been in just the state to pull a gun and blast off at the pair of them if he thought there was anything funny going on.'

'Yes, I suppose it does increase the probability of his guilt. But it doesn't make it certain,' said Antony firmly. 'Let's come up to date now, if you don't mind. When did you last see John Wilcox?'

'A couple of nights before the murder.'

'Could you be more exact?'

'It was the Monday,' Matty put in. 'And he was killed on Armistice Day, I remember, so it must have been the ninth.'

'That's right. They came to dinner here.'

'It's the same question, I'm afraid. How did Wilcox seem?'

'He wasn't a particularly excitable sort of chap, you know. I'd say he seemed much as usual.'

'Oh, but don't you remember, Fred, he started a conversation about whited sepulchres?'

'I don't remember, but no reason he shouldn't, that I can see.'

'It didn't seem like him, somehow. He really listened to our answers——'

'John always listened.'

'Yes, but not as if the answer meant something special to him.'

Maitland was intrigued. 'Can you remember anything more about that particular conversation, Mrs Tate?'

'Not really. Only that it surprised me. Fred was facetious about the subject, which John must have expected, but he didn't seem to like it for all that. And Martin ... no, I don't remember what he said.'

'The Roydons were present too?'

'Yes, we often get together like that, the six of us.'

'It would have been eight,' Tate put in, 'if Edward

and Madeleine were still alive. And now it will be only four.'

'Do you think,' said Maitland, with the sudden diffidence that could be so misleading, 'that the conversation could have been meant to have a particular application to somebody present?' ('You do ask the most damnable questions!' said Roger to him when they were on their way home.)

Neither of the Tates seemed to want to answer that. They exchanged glances, and at last Fred said, as though unwillingly, 'No, I don't think so. I really don't think so.'

'I see.' As though as an afterthought he added, 'By the way, what sort of a chap is Martin Roydon?'

'A good type. A cautious old bird, but a good type.'

'Very different from Fred,' said Matty, smiling as though she felt a sudden release from tension. 'I expect that's why they've always remained such good friends.'

Let it go at that? There didn't seem to be much choice. 'Did you see Mrs Wilcox recently?' Antony asked.

'Not since just after the trial, I'm afraid.' Matty seemed to have a better head for detail than her husband. 'We went to see her on the Saturday afternoon.'

'How did she take the verdict?'

'She was very bitter, but then she was very sure that Ellen had killed John. And that was awkward, because—' She broke off there, and seemed disinclined to continue.

'Because, Mrs Tate,' Antony prompted after a moment.

'Oh, I was going to say because William and Alison arrived just before we left. It was awkward, the way she felt, and their being so close to Ellen. Alison carried it off pretty well, luckily she was in one of her bright, chattery moods and didn't seem to notice anything wrong with the atmosphere. But poor William looked ready to die, I don't think he'd realised that Frances didn't accept the verdict.'

'To get back to Mrs Wilcox, was there anything—?'

'Not that question again!' Fred protested. 'There was nothing whatever that you wouldn't expect in the circumstances from a recently bereaved woman.' His manner was unusually vehement, and Antony glanced at Mrs Tate enquiringly.

'Do you agree with that?' he asked.

'Completely.'

'Then it only remains to ask you whether you, who knew these people so well, can suggest any motive for the murders.'

'If Edward didn't kill Madeleine ... but I find that hard to believe, I'm afraid.'

'Try,' Maitland urged.

Tate gave his boisterous laugh, not very appropriately. 'Nobody would have wanted to kill Madeleine,' he said, 'she was the most gentle soul alive. As for Foster, I didn't know him so well, but the motive Edward might have had certainly seems the most obvious.'

'Someone who might have wanted John Wilcox dead then, other than Ellen.'

'That's just as absurd. And if we're going on to Frances, I can't conceive of anyone, even Ellen, having a motive for killing her.'

'Then I think ... I can't think of anything more, can you, Roger?'

Roger, thus suddenly appealed to, didn't hesitate. 'There's one question that seems important,' he said. 'Do you know of any close relative of the Roydons who died of ... cancer, for instance? Something for which morphia might have been prescribed.'

Fred Tate looked from Farrell to Maitland and back again. 'That's plain speaking with a vengeance,' he said, 'because I suppose you'd like us to include our relations too. But no, I don't know of anybody in either family. Do you, Matty?'

This last question seemed to have been too much for Mrs Tate's composure. She said only, 'No,' but with nothing like her normal placidity. Antony got to his feet.

'You've been very patient with us,' he said, hiding his amusement at Roger's outspokenness even while he wondered if the answers had in any way represented the truth. 'We won't keep you any longer now.'

Tate showed them to the door. Even his exuberance seemed a trifle subdued, but he was laughing again, at a joke neither of them could see, as they made their way to the car.

They neither of them said much on the way home, except for a few desultory remarks. Antony promised to phone Roger the following morning, after he had spoken to Martin Roydon, and when they arrived in Kempenfeldt Square Roger said, 'I won't come in, it's late, and Meg will be ready before I get there if I don't hurry.' Meg's play, *Very Tragical Mirth* was having a rather stubborn run of success, due mainly to her personality, since the critics had hated the plot. 'This summer may finish it off,' Roger said hopefully as he was about to drive away, and Antony knew that Ellen Gray and all her works had momentarily been relegated to the back of his mind. He was always sanguine, when a play finished its run, that for a while he might have Meg to himself, without having to lose her daily into that world of shadows. And nearly always there was a new part waiting to engage her interest.

Antony was thinking of that, and not of the Tates at all, as he went into the hall and saw the study door standing ajar with the light within bearing testimony that his uncle was waiting for him. If it hadn't been so late Gibbs would no doubt have been hovering somewhere near to reinforce that mute summons, but of late years the old man had retired, with obstinate regularity, no later than ten o'clock.

So Maitland hesitated no more than a moment before he ignored the invitation of the staircase and crossed the hall to the open door. Against all precedent his uncle was on his feet to greet him, and as the younger man approached he brandished a piece of paper and said angrily, 'This would seem to be addressed to you.'

'May I see it, Uncle Nick?'

'Of course you may!' The paper was thrust into Antony's hand. 'It came through the letter box like that ... no envelope. Gibbs, very rightly, brought it to me.'

A scrap of paper apparently torn from an exercise book, and folded roughly square. The words MR MAIT-LAND were printed in large characters on one side. When he opened it out the message was printed too.

> DON'T THINK WE DON'T
> KNOW WHAT YOU'RE DOING
> YOU HAVE BEEN WARNED

'And what, may I ask,' said Sir Nicholas at his coldest, 'does that mean?'

SATURDAY, 6th February

I

He told Jenny about it the next morning at breakfast, it seemed the wisest thing to do. 'So I told him it was just someone who didn't like Ellen Gray,' he concluded. 'And he asked – just as you did, love – how they knew I was still interesting myself in her affairs?'

'Did you explain that to him?'

'Of course I didn't. I couldn't!' Antony protested. 'But it does make me think there may be more in these murders than appears on the surface.'

'But you always thought that, Antony.'

'Yes, but I was thinking of something personal. This seems more ... well, it makes you think, doesn't it?'

Jenny smiled at him. 'You said that before,' she reminded him. 'What it makes me think, Antony, is that you ought to be very careful.'

'That goes for you too. That's why I told you,' he admitted. 'And while I'm about it I'd better tell you what happened on Thursday night as Roger and I were coming home.'

'Something else?' asked Jenny apprehensively.

'More of the same, that's all. Two men stopped us in the square and told us to leave Ellen Gray's affairs alone, or words to that effect.'

'Antony—'

'So you'll be careful, love. I know you're not silly enough to be taken in by a fake message—'

'Things that might have been expressed differently,' murmured Jenny irrepressibly.

'—but there's nothing to be lost by taking the warnings seriously.'

'Oh, I do, Antony ... for you. I'm quite safe here, and when I go out I don't suppose "they" know me by sight. But it's different—'

'Jenny love, you'll make me sorry I told you.'

'Then I won't say any more.' But she couldn't quite bring herself to leave the subject. 'You and Roger, you're one as bad as the other for being secretive,' she grumbled.

'That was what was biting Uncle Nick, of course,' he told her. 'That I hadn't told him anything about the previous warnings, I mean.'

Once the meal was cleared away Antony settled himself down to telephone. He called Martin Roydon first and made an appointment for that afternoon, called Roger to confirm the time, and then dialled Doctor Clive's number. It was Alison who answered the phone, and there was a short delay in producing the doctor. 'You caught me just as I was going out,' said William Clive.

'I won't keep you long. But I admit to being curious; have the police finished their examination of your records?'

'They have. It was as I told you, there was nothing wrong.'

'Well, that's a relief, anyway.'

'It does not seem to have altogether quieted Inspector Conway's suspicions, however.'

'That's a pity. Has something else happened?'

'The police came armed with a warrant and searched the house from top to bottom.'

'What were they looking for?'

'A diary of John Wilcox's that Barbara says is missing.'

173

'It's rather late in the day for that to be noticed surely.'

'I'm not quite clear about that, or why it should be considered important.'

'Then I must ask Barbara myself. Tell me, doctor, about the morphine. Have you been able to gather from the police whether it was taken orally or given by means of an injection?'

'It was given orally.'

'I ought to have known that, I suppose. Even Conway would hardly suspect that Frances Wilcox had allowed Ellen to give her an injection. Have you any idea in what quantity—?'

'The inspector has not confided in me. I don't know if you know anything about morphine poisoning.'

'I've been looking it up. Even one grain may be considered dangerous to someone who is not an addict, but on the other hand people have been known to recover after as much as sixty grains. In general, however, three grains would constitute a fatal dose.'

'That coincides with my own researches into the subject.' The doctor sounded faintly amused. 'I don't see how Ellen could be expected to have known; but there, I suppose Inspector Conway would say she had access to my text books if she wished to make use of them.'

'He won't arrest her, however, unless he discovers some source from which the morphine might have come,' said Antony positively. 'Unless, of course—'

'That's something to be thankful for, anyway,' said William Clive, not waiting for him to finish. 'But, Mr Maitland, I really must be going.'

'Yes, of course. I'm sorry to have delayed you.' He rang off, paused for a moment with his hand still on the receiver, and then reached for the telephone book. When he had found the number he wanted he wrote it down, and still did not place the call immediately. Barbara Wilcox would still be in some distress over her mother's death, and he hesitated to intrude on her. On the other hand, there wasn't a hope of getting the information he wanted from Inspector Conway ...

When he finally dialled the Wilcoxes' number, the phone rang for some time unanswered, and he was just about to hang up when he heard the receiver removed at the other end and Barbara Wilcox's voice came to him faintly. 'Hallo.'

'Miss Wilcox?'

'Yes.' Her voice came through more strongly now. 'Who is that?' she asked, a little sharply.

'Antony Maitland. I appreciate that you don't want to be troubled at a time like this, Miss Wilcox—'

'I don't want to talk to you.'

'Please!'

'You came to see my mother, and your visit worried her frightfully. And then next day she was dead.'

'Don't you care at all that Ellen may be accused again of murder, and again – as I think – unfairly?'

'That has nothing to do with me.' Her voice sounded hard, and far older than seventeen, but she didn't ring off, and he took heart from that.

'I only want you to answer one question for me,' he pleaded.

He thought perhaps it was curiosity as much as anything else that prompted her to reply, 'What is it?'

'What do you know of a diary that the police say is missing?'

'Nothing much. I don't see how it can be important. It was my father's. I don't mean Dad kept a regular diary, just a current one for engagements and things, and then he'd throw it away at the end of the year.'

'I see. When did you notice it was missing?'

'It was like this.' Her sigh was impatient, but she went on answering. Perhaps, after all, it was merely that any distraction was better than none. 'Nobody looked for it

175

after Dad died, but then Mother found it one day pushed behind another row of books in the drawing-room.'

'Do you remember what day that was?'

'The day before – the day before she died.' Now there was no doubt about it; she wasn't the self-possessed woman she was trying to sound but a young girl who was bitterly unhappy.

'Is your brother there?' he asked.

'Yes, but ... he won't want to talk to you, Mr Mait-land.'

'That doesn't matter. It was just—'

'My aunt and uncle are here too. My mother's brother and his wife.'

'That's good. I'm sure you know, Miss Wilcox, that you have my sympathy in your loss.'

She said, surprised, 'I believe you mean that.'

'I do. And I wouldn't be worrying you if it weren't really important.'

'No, I see.' Somehow over that unsympathetic instrument, the telephone, they had established a rapport. He spoke quietly, thinking that any ill-chosen word might break the link.

'You say your mother found the diary.'

'Yes, and she was a bit puzzled, because why should he have put it there? There was nothing private about it. She opened it, and riffled through the pages; she'd been looking for a book to take to bed. And she said, "I'll take this up with me as well, in case Dad wrote any-thing", but she said it casually, not really thinking there might be anything there. And next morning it was on her bedside table when I took in her morning tea. But afterwards it was gone.'

'And you never looked in it yourself?'

'No. Do you think, Mr Maitland, there might be some-thing there?'

'Well, it's odd that it should go missing again. And it would account ... Miss Wilcox! I can't talk this over with you without upsetting you, and I don't want to do that.'

'All right.' She sounded almost submissive now. 'But some day will you tell me—?'

'When I know more, if I ever do,' he promised. And exchanged farewells, contrary to all expectations, in a glow of friendliness.

II

Martin and Dorothy Roydon lived in Streatham, in a large, old house only a few minutes' walk from the common. One look at Martin was sufficient to convince Maitland that the impression he had gained at the trial was a true one; he'd have to be careful how he put his questions if he didn't want to antagonise the other man hopelessly. He glanced at Roger, wishing he had thought to mention the matter during the drive out; but then consoled himself with the thought that Roger was quite as sensitive to atmosphere as he was himself, and wasn't likely to put a foot wrong.

Dorothy Roydon was another matter. She was small, and fair, and very pale, and didn't look as though she would take umbrage at even the most outrageous of questions. But perhaps not altogether the nonentity that Alison Clive had called her. It might have been interesting and instructive to talk to her alone, but it was too late to worry about that now.

The furniture in the drawing-room was old, though by no means antique, the wood surfaces well polished, and everything meticulously in place. 'The first thing,' said Martin, when they were all seated round the hearth, 'is for you to explain to us why you are here.'

'May I ask you a question in return? You gave evidence on Ellen Gray's behalf. How did you feel about it?'

'Ambivalent, Mr Maitland, if that's any help to you.'

'I see. You have, or had some affection for her, didn't you?'

'Certainly. I don't know, though, whether that affection can survive many more knocks.'

'What do you mean?'

'I've heard what happened to Frances Wilcox. Doctor Clive told me, and also that the police are again asking questions of Ellen.'

'Did he also tell you that I was still interested in the case?'

'Not that, no.'

'Do you really think it's likely that Ellen should have killed Mrs Wilcox?'

'If there was some motive arising out of John's murder ... oh, I don't know what to think.'

'I agree, it's difficult. What do you think about it, Mrs Roydon?' he asked, turning to her suddenly.

'I should very much like to believe that Ellen is innocent.'

'Then you can't object to my trying to prove it,' he said rather as though her admission constituted a major victory. 'To answer your question a little more fully, Mr Roydon, I believe that not only are the two recent murders connected but that the murders of Madeleine Gray and Michael Foster should be reconsidered as well. I mean that the motive for John Wilcox's killing arose from the former case, and that his death, in turn, provided the motive for his wife's murder.'

'But Edward Gray is dead,' said Roydon, as if he found the whole idea that Maitland was presenting completely inconceivable.

'Exactly. But if the three murders are connected, the

murderer must be looked for among the people who knew both families then, and now.'

'Such as myself, for instance,' said Roydon, very quietly. His wife leaned forward and said with some agitation,

'I'm sure Mr Maitland didn't mean anything of the kind.'

'But I did.' Now what had possessed him, after all his good resolutions, to go straight to the heart of the matter like that? He hardly thought Dorothy's intervention would have a mellowing effect on her husband. 'Yourself, or Mr Tate. You're the only surviving members of the group, aren't you? I gathered as much from Mrs Wilcox before she died.'

'You mean that Frances—?' Roydon sounded stunned.

'No, I'm sorry if I misled you. She was very fervent in her belief in Ellen's guilt. But she talked of "the clique", and naturally I was interested.'

'If you think you can prove after all these years that somebody else – not Edward – killed those two ... you're mad!' said Martin with conviction.

'Very possibly. But I've explained myself very frankly, Mr Roydon. Are you prepared to answer my questions?'

'I don't know,' Roydon began, and then an odd thing happened. Dorothy Roydon put a hand on her husband's arm to attract his attention, and when he turned to look at her said, 'Yes, Martin,' in a low, breathless voice.

It was even odder, to Antony's mind, that after a moment's pause Martin smiled at her and said without a hint of impatience, 'Now why should you want me to do that?'

'Because we're fond of Ellen, you know we are.'

'But it's as good as saying ... I know I haven't killed anybody, but it's as good as agreeing that Fred may have.'

'I don't look at it that way at all. If it will set Mr

179

Maitland's mind at rest, that neither of you—'

'I see what you mean.' He turned to look at Antony again. 'I seem to have been outvoted,' he said wryly. 'So go ahead.'

'Then we'll start with what happened nineteen, nearly twenty years ago. Do you remember the night Edward Gray came home?'

'I only heard what had happened afterwards, you know,' said Roydon obliquely.

'I understand that. You were stationed at Uxbridge, weren't you?'

'You seem to be well informed.'

'Mr Tate told me that. Also that he was on leave and was expecting you that evening in town, but at the last minute you couldn't get away.'

'His memory is better than mine then. But there wasn't likely to be any extra duty going at that date, if I let him down most likely it was a girl. I didn't meet Dorothy until the war was over.'

'I see. You knew Madeleine Gray though. Did you know Michael Foster too?'

'Only as a recent acquaintance. He was around rather a lot when I went to see Madeleine.'

'Did you get the impression that there was anything between them?'

'N-no. But I don't think I'm very observant about things like that. I wasn't surprised when I heard.'

'You weren't surprised that Edward—'

'He'd been through hell in the Far East, and his temper wasn't too stable at the best of times. I've never had any doubt that he was guilty, and I've never blamed him all that much either, if you want to know.'

'What was Foster like?'

'A quiet chap with a nice sense of humour. Looking back, I can quite see that Madeleine might have been attracted to him.'

'When was the last time you saw her?'

'Not long before she died. The Sunday before, I believe. Fred was there too.

'But not Foster?'

'No.'

'Did you notice anything different about her that day?'

'That's funny,' Roydon said slowly. 'She wanted advice ... something that was worrying her.'

'Your advice and Tate's?'

'No, mine. When she let me in she whispered, "Stay after Fred has gone if you can". So I did.'

'Don't keep me in suspense, Mr Roydon. What was troubling her?'

'I haven't thought about it from that day to this. It seemed to be a matter of conscience. What did you do if someone you were fond of was doing something dreadful and you found out about it?'

'And what did you advise her?'

'I said I thought it depended on how fond she was of the person concerned, and she said – let me get this right – "Very fond, very grateful". So I told her in that case I should talk to the person concerned and try to persuade them to stop doing ... whatever it was.'

'It didn't occur to you afterwards that the conversation might have been significant?'

'No, and I don't really see it now. Your asking me that – was anything different? – brought it to mind, but the case against Edward was so very clear cut, you know.'

'Not an isolated case. I suppose that inclined you to believe it. When did you last see Edward Gray?'

'It must have been the leave before he went missing, before he was sent east. I don't really remember.'

'Did you attend the trial?'

'I was there the last two days, I'd managed to wangle some leave.'

'Any surprises there?'

181

'Only that he went on denying what seemed so obvious.'

'You know what had happened to him during the six months he was missing?'

'Of course I do. John told me. I think I said before that it only made it seem more likely—' He broke off there. 'I still can't believe you about that, you know,' he added after a moment.

'We'll come to last November, then. When did you last see John Wilcox?'

'Two days before he was killed. We dined with the Tates, and John and Frances were there.'

'Anything particular about that evening?'

'I thought John seemed jumpy,' said Dorothy unexpectedly.

'You're being wise after the event,' said Martin, smiling at her. 'Everything was just as usual.'

'Do you remember a conversation about whited sepulchres?' Antony asked them.

'Now you mention it ... but what on earth could that have to do with John's murder?' Martin demanded.

'Perhaps nothing, perhaps everything,' Maitland told him. 'If you could tell me—'

'Well, it was all rather vague really. Didn't you think so, Dorothy? John said something about not being able to judge by appearances, and I think it was Fred who said "whited sepulchres", as a joke, you know. But John was perfectly serious.'

'What was your own contribution to the subject, Mr Roydon?'

'I can't remember that I had anything to say about it at all.'

'It was all so vague,' said Dorothy, repeating her husband's word.

'Then perhaps you won't be able to answer my next question, but I think I'll ask it all the same. Could Mr

Wilcox's rather pointed remarks have been aimed at somebody present?'

'It never occurred to me, and it doesn't occur to me now,' said Roydon, more forcefully than he had previously spoken.

'I'm sorry,' said Antony, answering the tone rather than the words. 'So we come to Mrs Wilcox. When did you last see her?'

'The Sunday after the trial ended. She was upset by the verdict, you know.'

'So I gather.'

'But I saw her last Wednesday,' Dorothy put in. 'And if you're going to ask if there was anything strange about her manner, Mr Maitland, Frances was always worried about something. But there was nothing out of the way.'

'I see. Then there only remain two questions. The first is, can you think of anyone who might have a motive for these murders? And I do want to stress that it's important; you shouldn't let your loyalties blind you.'

'But there's nothing!' Dorothy protested. Her husband said more slowly,

'I have to agree with that. For instance, it was the sheer – the sheer unmurderability of Madeleine and Michael Foster that made it so easy to believe in Edward's guilt.'

'And that goes for John and Frances too,' added Dorothy.

'But if one thing led to another ... well, it's no use speculating. And that brings me to the last question, which is one you may not like,' – but there was no way of wrapping it up, was there? – 'Did any member of the Tates' family die of cancer, for instance? Something for which morphine might have been prescribed.' And that, so far as he could remember, was exactly what Roger had put to the Tates, with only the change of name.

183

'And I suppose you asked Fred and Matty the same question about us,' said Roydon, as though he had been reading Antony's mind. Oddly he sounded merely thoughtful, not particularly put out at all.

'You know, then, that I've been to see them already?'

'Oh, yes, Fred phoned me as soon as you left. He was a bit excited, though, I never gathered exactly what it was you wanted.'

'That doesn't answer my question, Mr Roydon.'

'It's easily answered. Nobody in our family; and I don't know of anybody related to Fred and Matty, and I think I should know.'

'Very well then. I'm grateful to you both.'

'What will happen now? Will Ellen be arrested?'

'Not unless they find some further evidence. Which they very well may do,' he added to Roger when they had made their farewells and were back in the car again. Roger made no immediate reply, and it was not until they had joined the stream of traffic up the High Street that he said,

'Is that a prophecy?'

'What? Oh, evidence! There was something about fingerprints, if you remember. And there was something about Ellen's story of what she was doing on Thursday afternoon that I didn't altogether like.'

'Are you changing your mind about her?'

'I've changed it a dozen times,' said Antony gloomily. 'But if you ask me if I think she's innocent—'

'I should be interested to know.'

'Well, I do. I think someone – not Edward – killed Madeleine Gray and Michael Foster all that time ago, and that that led to what has been happening recently.'

'If somebody knew too much why wait nineteen years—?'

'I don't know. Perhaps it was only that the same motive resurrected itself.'

'And what was the motive?'

'I'm beginning to have a very good idea.'

'Well?' said Roger rather sharply, after the silence had lengthened a little.

'Something to do with drugs,' said Antony vaguely.

'If you deduce that from the mere fact that somebody gave Frances Wilcox morphine—'

'It had to come from somewhere,' Maitland pointed out.

'Granted, but—'

'There are also our friends, whom we met in the square the other night.'

'*And* the telephone call, *and* the anonymous letter,' said Roger. 'All those things may be connected—'

'I'm sure they are.'

'—but there's nothing to tie them in with – with a drug racket, I suppose you mean.'

'Something like that,' said Antony, vague again. 'Tell me, what did you think of the Roydons?'

'I liked him, and from what you told me I didn't expect to. As for her, she's one of the quiet sort who gets her own way more often than not, I should think.'

'That was my impression too.' He glanced at his watch, and then stretched luxuriously. 'What's more important at the moment, Roger, is that Jenny will have tea ready by the time we get home.'

III

When Antony opened the door from the landing to the upper hall, the telephone was ringing. By the time he reached the living-room Jenny was standing with the receiver in her hand. 'It's for you, Antony. Inspector Conway ... I think.' The detective had a bad habit of not announcing himself.

Maitland went across to the writing-table in the corner, where the telephone stood, merely pausing on the way to raise a hand in greeting to Meg. When he had said, 'Maitland here,' and Conway had identified himself rather as if he were giving away a state secret, the inspector added,

'I've something to tell you, Mr Maitland.'

'That's good.' To say he was surprised would be to put it mildly, but nothing of that appeared in his voice.

'Those two men you told me about—'

'Don't tell me you've found out who they are!'

'I think so.' Conway's tone was enough to repress any enthusiasm. 'And I'm forced to the conclusion that you didn't tell me the exact truth about that incident, Mr Maitland.'

Antony suppressed an instinct to retort angrily. 'Truth isn't truth unless it's exact,' he pointed out.

'If you will let me speak!' said Conway, so that Antony was reminded, immediately and irrelevantly, of the judge in *Trial by Jury*, and straight away put into a good humour again.

'Fire away,' he said, by way of encouragement.

'The car belonged to Jack Bellamy, who is known to us; the shorter of the two men you described to me might well have been him. The other description fits well enough one of his known associates, a man called Douglas, or Doug Armitage.'

'And their line of business, Inspector?' When Conway did not reply immediately he went on, 'If you don't want to tell me I'll make a guess. I'd say they were connected with the drug trade.'

'Then you do know more than you told me,' said Conway furiously.

'Am I right?'

'I think you know that you are.'

'No, it was as I said, a guess.'

186

'I don't believe you!'

'Perhaps if Conway hadn't lost his temper his own would have been gone irretrievably. As it was he said, quite mildly, 'All the same, it's the truth.'

'And nothing to do with Ellen Gray,' said Conway, ignoring the statement.

'As to that, I can only tell you what they told me.'

'There can be no possible connection.'

'I should tell you that there have been other incidents. A telephone call that specifically mentioned her, and warned me not to interfere; and an anonymous letter that, taken in conjunction with the other things, could only have been meant to convey the same threat.'

'Is all this intended to convince me of your client's innocence?' enquired Conway sarcastically.

'She isn't my client now.'

'If you must be so precise!' Conway was irritated again. 'As for your precious Miss Gray—'

'Yes?' prompted Antony, when some instinct of caution caused Conway to hesitate.

'I have a warrant for her arrest,' snapped the inspector.

'Some new evidence then?'

'Evidence enough.'

'The fingerprints?'

'That's only part of it.'

'What then?' Conway wouldn't answer that, he was sure of it, but the detective went on without any hesitation.

'She was seen in Bayswater in the afternoon of the day Frances Wilcox died.'

'That's hard to believe, Inspector.'

'It's true enough, for all that. Seen and recognised by a neighbour who knew her when she used to baby-sit for the Wilcox children.' Conway didn't actually add,

So there! but Antony felt he might just as well have done so.

He said, 'When—?'

'In due course,' said Conway stiffly, not pretending to misunderstand him. And rang off firmly before anything more could be said.

Antony turned from the phone. 'Roger, I'm sorry, will you take me to Roehampton right away? I want to see Ellen Gray.'

'Something's happened,' said Jenny, who had just come in with the tea-pot.

'Conway's going to arrest her.'

'When?'

'He didn't say. Only, "in due course". But I must see her first.'

'Not even time for tea, darling?' asked Meg.

'No time for anything. Jenny, when we've gone, will you phone Geoffrey?' He had reached the door by this time, and when there came a knock on the outer door he went quickly across the hall to answer it. Gibbs stood on the landing with a look of long-suffering on his face and a sheaf of yellow tulips wrapped in green paper in his hand.

'For Mrs Maitland,' he said.

'Yes, thank you, Gibbs.' No use adding, 'If you'd used the house phone one of us would have come down for them.' Antony took the flowers and went back into the living-room. 'For you, love,' he said.

'Who on earth—?'

'Somebody a bit late for your wedding anniversary,' Meg suggested.

'Perhaps.' Jenny had found the card by now, and as she read it all the colour drained out of her face. 'Antony,' she said. 'Look!'

He took the card from her. Rough printing that he thought he recognised. ENJOY THE FLOWERS, MRS MAIT-

188

LAND. NEXT TIME IT MIGHT BE A BOMB. 'Hell and d-damna-
tion,' he said in a strangled voice. And then, 'This is the
l-last thing that will h-happen, Jenny. We'll f-finish this
now!'

Meg was saying, 'Let me see.' He held the card out
to her, holding it by its edges, so that both the Farrells
could read it. Roger, who had been inclined to enter a
protest against what he had felt to be an excessive reaction, swore himself, and then was silent.

'What now?' Meg asked.

'To R-roehampton, as I s-said.'

'Oughtn't you to tell the police?'

'It's m-more important to s-see Ellen.'

He was talking in a hurried way, very unlike himself,
and the stammer that only afflicted him when he was
angry was more marked than any of them had ever heard
it. Roger found his voice then and said, 'Calm down,
Antony,' but Maitland took no notice. He was too intent
on the instructions he was giving.

'Jenny and M-meg, you stay here. I don't w-want
either of you to go out on any account whatever. I'll tell
G-gibbs ... no, I won't, I'll t-tell Uncle N-nick and he'll
tell Gibbs that n-nobody is to be admitted, n-nothing
taken in. Now I think of it, he can ring the p-police too.'

'If you're not back before I leave for the theatre—'
said Meg. The hint of uncertainty in her voice was also
uncharacteristic.

'You'll l-let your understudy go on. I m-mean that,
Meg.'

'All right.' She sounded docile, and he looked at her
suspiciously. 'I mean it too, darling,' she said, smiling
at him. 'Do you think I'd leave Jenny alone?'

'The thing is,' said Jenny, 'what are *you* going to do?'

'T-talk to Ellen Gray, d-damn her,' said Antony, and
disappeared through the doorway with Roger in close
pursuit.

IV

By the time they got downstairs Antony was sufficiently master of himself to control his stammer while he talked to Sir Nicholas. Which was just as well, because otherwise they would have been delayed while his uncle spoke his mind, and he was still in a tearing hurry, though trying not to show it. The journey to Roehampton was accomplished in rather a grim silence, which was hard on Roger who had a hundred questions he wanted to ask. In addition, he mistrusted his friend's mood and would have been glad enough to try to talk him out of it if he hadn't felt that any effort in that direction would only make matters worse. So he concentrated on reaching their destination as quickly as the traffic would allow, and was relieved when Antony spoke to him in his ordinary voice when they drew up outside the Clives' house behind the two cars that were already parked there.

'At least Conway isn't here before us.' One of the cars was large and opulent, the other small and sporty; neither of them resembled a police car in any way.

'Is that so important?'

'It is.'

'Shall I wait?'

'No, come with me, Roger. I may need a witness.'

The door was opened to them by Alison Clive. She looked pale, and a little bit trembly, and Roger wondered briefly what was wrong with her. But Maitland swept on to his point after the barest civilities. 'We want to see Miss Gray.' And added, as if the idea had only just occurred to him, 'Don't tell me she's out.'

'No, she's at home. She and Stephen are in the dining-room,' said Alison, backing away from the door so that they could enter. 'I hope you won't want to disturb Will. He's at home, too, but he has a friend with him.'

Antony wasn't committing himself. 'Just Miss Gray for the moment,' he said. 'The dining-room ... is that the door over there?'

'That's right. Shall I tell her——?'

'No need, Mrs Clive. I don't think she'll be altogether surprised to see me.' He went across to the door he had indicated as he spoke, waited until Roger caught up with him, and then opened it and went in. 'I'm sorry to disturb you, Miss Gray,' he said. Roger thought he had never heard a statement so blatantly insincere.

There was a long dining-table, with chairs that might have been Chippendale. Ellen and Stephen Langland were seated by the fireplace at the far side of the room, which must have been centrally heated, because there was no fire in the grate. Stephen got to his feet as the two newcomers crossed the room, and if he was surprised he didn't show it.

'Have you got some good news for us, Mr Maitland?' he said.

Antony came to a halt. 'Nothing but the worst,' he said. 'But before that happens I want to talk to Miss Gray.'

'I don't understand. Before what happens?'

'There's a warrant out for her arrest.' The words were addressed to Stephen, but he was watching Ellen as he spoke. She had looked peaceful when they came in, he thought, and nothing much happened now except that her expression hardened a little.

'For murdering Frances?' she said in a brittle voice.

'That's right. But before Conway gets here——'

'Today?'

'I'm not sure. Very likely. I want you to answer one question for me, Miss Gray.'

'There can't be anything left to tell you, surely.'

'If you think a little you'll realise that isn't true,'

191

he told her. 'And I should have said, two questions, but one is more important than the other.'

'Well?'

'You've been m-making a f-fool of me quite long enough,' Maitland said, and Roger at least realised that his temper was being held, with difficulty, on a tight rein.

Stephen said, 'Look here—' rather ineffectually. And Ellen said angrily,

'I don't know what you mean!'

'I mean that you've n-never answered the q-question I asked you the first time I saw you, when you were in p-prison awaiting trial.'

'What question?'

'Whom, or what you saw when you arrived at the flat in B-bayswater on the evening John Wilcox was killed?'

'I didn't see *anybody*.' The emphasis was slight, but enough for Maitland, who pounced on it as if it had been an admission.

'Some*thing* then?'

'No.'

'Miss Gray, I'm trying to help you. Is it fair to lie to me?'

'I'm not lying.'

'Ellen doesn't tell lies.' That was Stephen, who had crossed the hearth to sit on the arm of Ellen's chair.

'If you really think that, I'm afraid you're going to be disillusioned, Mr Langland. There was at least one other lie she told.'

'I don't believe you.'

'Ask her yourself. Why didn't you tell me you were in Bayswater on Thursday afternoon, Miss Gray, not long before Frances Wilcox died?'

She looked up at him then and said, with a candid air, 'Because I thought you'd insist on my telling the police, and it was none of their business.'

'I hope you can convince a jury of that.'

'I don't see how I could. I don't see how I can face ... all that ... again.' Stephen's arm went round her shoulders.

'Why did you go there?' he asked quietly, as though he was afraid of startling her.

'Because I wanted to straighten things out with Frances. I couldn't bear her still thinking that I'd killed John. But I rang the bell and rang the bell, and then I knocked on the door, but there was no reply.'

'You're forgetting one thing, Miss Gray. Your fingerprints were found in the room where Mrs Wilcox died.'

'Well ... I did go in.'

'How? It isn't possible that you should still have the keys.'

'The doors were open. I mean, not latched. So I thought I'd see if Frances was there, lying down perhaps, so that she hadn't heard me. I really did want to put things right with her.'

'And what did you find?'

'It was horrible.'

'Never mind that. T-tell me.'

'Frances was lying on the floor, as though she'd been trying to get to the door when she died. I turned her over to – to see if there was anything I could do for her, and she looked quite peaceful, only her face was blue and pinched as if she was cold. And she was cold, Mr Maitland, I don't think she'd just died.'

'I see. You realise, of course, that the prosecution will maintain she must have been alive when you got there, to let you in.'

'Yes. I realise that.'

'So you left without taking any action. It didn't occur to you that you should call the police?'

'I knew what they'd think.'

'Is that the truth this time?' Maitland asked.

'Of course it's the truth,' said Stephen indignantly.

'There is still the other question.'

'Which she has answered.'

'I thought you were on my side,' said Ellen, rather tremulously.

'I am on your s-side. Wholeheartedly on your side now. Look here, Miss Gray,' – he was making a real effort at self-control – 'if you won't tell me for your own sake think of ... Mr Langland, for instance. Doesn't he deserve your consideration?' She made no answer to that, only looked at him in silence while two large tears coursed down her cheeks, and Antony hardened his heart and set himself deliberately to play on her emotions. 'When you told me you were going back to work you meant – didn't you? – that you weren't going to keep Mr Langland at arm's length any longer. Perhaps even that you were going to agree to being engaged to him.'

'Yes, I meant all that.' She put up a hand to touch Stephen's where it lay on her shoulder. 'It was ... you made me see I should fight. But now I'm afraid it wasn't fair of me.'

'Of course we should be engaged. Whatever happens, I'm with you, Ellen.'

'You can't go to prison with her,' Maitland pointed out, rather acidly. Then he turned back to the girl again. 'You made your choice, Miss Gray,' he said. 'Whatever you do now he's going to get hurt ... don't you understand that? It isn't easy to stand by and watch someone you love—'

'You're not being fair to me, Mr Maitland.' There were more tears now, and she dashed a hand angrily across her eyes. 'You say I'm going to be arrested again, and what I told you about being in Bayswater can only make matters worse.'

'There is the other question. The answer to that might make all the difference.'

'But, I—'

'Yes, I know it's hard.' For the first time there was sympathy in his voice. 'But sometimes old loyalties have to give way to new ones, you know.'

Stephen was silent now. Only his hand on Ellen's shoulder had tightened its grip, and he had pulled her against him almost angrily.

'He's always been so good to me,' said Ellen.

'Yes, I know. But I'd like the others to hear: Mr Farrell and Mr Langland. Who has been good to you?'

'I don't think you need me to tell you, Mr Maitland. Uncle Will.'

'So it was Doctor Clive you saw in Bayswater?'

'No, that was the truth at least. His car was parked a few doors away. I watched him drive off, but I couldn't actually see him from where I was. But, Mr Maitland, it can only have been a coincidence.'

'Does he have patients as far afield as Bayswater? Or any friends there other than John and Frances Wilcox? No, I don't think it was precisely a coincidence, Miss Gray.'

'I'll never believe—'

'And that being so,' Antony went on as though she hadn't spoken, 'I think we'll just have a word with him.'

'There's someone with him. Or there was when Stephen arrived.'

'A friend?'

'I've seen him before, but Uncle Will never introduced us. Mr Maitland, you can't—'

'Can't I? We'll s-see about that. You'd better stay here, Roger. There may be trouble over this.'

'All the more reason—'

'No.'

'Don't argue with me, Antony. You said you wanted a witness.'

'Well, I do, but—'

'That's settled, then.' He was already on his way to the door. 'Are you going to wait, or throw the visitor out?'

'We'll see. At least, I mean, we're not going to wait, but it may not be necessary—' They were in the hall now. He thought Ellen was still protesting, but he ignored that as he had ignored her previous interruption. The door to the drawing-room was closed, but as he went nearer he could distinguish the deep tones of Doctor Clive and a lighter voice that he thought he recognised as that of the man who had telephoned him three evenings before and refused to give his name. 'It's all right, Roger. At least, I think it is,' he said, and threw open the door as he spoke.

Doctor Clive, who had been sitting with his back to the door, came to his feet and spun round to see the source of the interruption. 'Mr Maitland! This is quite unforgivable,' he exclaimed, but Antony had only a passing interest in the anger in his voice, the first signs of such an emotion he had ever seen in him. His eyes went past the doctor to the other man who was sitting, very much at his ease, at the other side of the hearth.

'Won't you introduce me,' he said, 'to your f-friend.'

'Certainly not. You have no right.' But the stranger spoke then, and now there could be no doubt about it, it was the cultured voice he had heard before.

'So this is Mr Maitland. I am happy to make your acquaintance.' He was a slim man, fair, almost bleached looking, with a thin face and very cold blue eyes.

'We are already acquainted, after a f-fashion, I believe,' said Antony, barely controlling his temper. Roger, who had been completely mystified up to this point, made a wild guess as to the reason, and chanced upon the right one. He also began to see, or thought he did, what his friend had meant by "trouble". He glanced

196

at the door, wondering whether Ellen and Stephen had followed them, but it was tightly shut and they, presumably, had gone back to the dining-room.

'Now, how do you make that out?' the stranger was saying.

'Your v-voice is quite unmistakable.'

'A pity. Or perhaps not. Would it be too much to ask you to explain why you broke in on our conversation so rudely? I don't object, you must understand, but Doctor Clive seems quite put out.'

Maitland was in the middle of the room now, with Roger at his elbow. He looked down at the stranger, and Doctor Clive, who had found himself ignored since his early protest, flung himself back in his chair again.

'You th-threatened me,' said Maitland. 'That I can f-for-give. But you b-brought my wife into it b-by your action today, and that's something I w-won't s-stand for.'

'That's odd,' said the fair man thoughtfully. 'I thought the flowers were a nice touch, myself. Now if you'd said that you found my – er – my henchmen a little crude in their ways I could understand it. And this is your friend who was with you?' The cold eyes rested on Roger for a moment. 'It's a pity he should have been brought into the matter, but it can't be helped now.'

'Into what?'

'You haven't asked me the subject of our conversation, though I am sure you would have got round to it in a moment. I find your methods, Mr Maitland, disconcertingly direct.'

'D-does that make it my t-turn to apologise? What was the subject of your conversation with Doctor Clive, then?'

'Why, how to dispose of you, my dear fellow, since it seems you don't intend to heed my warnings. And of your friend, of course, since you were so inconsiderate as to bring him with you.'

'I see. Had you reached any conclusions?'

'If we had, all that is altered now. Since you have met me ... and that reminds me, Mr Maitland, you didn't seem surprised to find me here. Now, that I find rather odd.'

'It was a stroke of luck I hadn't bargained for. But I've come to certain conclusions about Doctor Clive, and your own activities led me to postulate some connection between you.'

'That's very interesting. I wonder if you will continue to consider it "a stroke of luck", however.'

'If you're thinking of murdering us,' said Antony, almost good-humouredly, 'I really don't think it's a good idea. How would Doctor Clive deal with the situation, for instance?' William Clive gave something very like a moan, and Maitland turned to him with a show of sympathy. 'Yes, I thought you'd agree with me, doctor,' he said.

'You under-rate me, Mr Maitland,' said the stranger sharply, almost as though he didn't like losing the attention of his audience even for a moment. 'It would not, of course, be feasible to kill you here and now, but there would be nothing more simple than for me to arrange that you did not reach home alive. And that is exactly what I intend to do.'

'You're forgetting there might be some questions asked.'

'But not of me, and not of my friend William.'

'The police—'

'Know nothing of those conclusions you spoke of. Am I not right?'

'No.'

'Come now, Mr Maitland,' – Doctor Clive seemed to have taken some heart from this last exchange – 'you are hardly on confidential terms with Inspector Conway, judging from what I heard here the other night.'

198

'I've only to reach a telephone box—'

'An excellent idea,' said the stranger enthusiastically. 'It would ensure the success of my plans. A sitting target, and your friend waiting for you—'

'If we decide to hold you here until the police can be called—'

'I should not allow it. Are you armed? I thought not.' A small, but ugly-looking pistol appeared in his hand.

'You daren't use it,' said Antony positively.

'I should regret having to do so, certainly. It would make difficulties, as you have pointed out. But it is a matter of degree. Frankly, Mr Maitland, you are too dangerous to me alive.'

'I see. Keep still, Roger!' he added, as Roger moved restlessly at his side. 'This chap means what he's saying.' Roger subsided with a murmured protest, but the thought was in both their minds, though unspoken, 'A little later ... when he's off his guard—' But the fair man looked distressingly alert.

'I'm glad you show so much good sense,' he said now, in a congratulatory tone. And, as if he had divined their thought, 'Won't you both sit down, for the time being. There are things I'd like to know.'

'On the whole,' said Antony, 'I'd rather stand.' He wasn't under any illusions that the stranger wouldn't see through this desire on his part, so he wasn't particularly upset to meet a distinctly derisory look.

'As you will. Don't expect me to grow careless though. I shan't.'

'I don't expect it,' said Antony in a despairing tone. (If anything had been needed to ready Roger for action, it would have been that.)

The fair man gave him a sharp, enquiring look, but said only, 'I've heard of you, Mr Maitland.' And at that moment, as if on a cue, they heard the doorbell shrilling somewhere at the back of the house. Doctor Clive came clumsily to his feet. Of the four men in the room, he was by far the least calm.

'I'll get rid of whoever it is,' he muttered.

'I don't think you'll be able to,' said Antony, playing a hunch. 'And I should put that plaything away if I were you,' he added, with a rather sardonic glance in the stranger's direction. 'If I'm not mistaken, that's the police.'

The gun had disappeared as if it had never been. 'So you did communicate with Inspector Conway,' said the fair man harshly.

'If you want the truth, he communicated with me ... his intention of arresting Miss Gray.'

'Then let him get on with it!'

'Oh, no. I don't think you'll use your pistol, you know, not just at the moment.' He was making for the door as he spoke. Roger, moving quietly and not saying anything, went to stand behind the stranger's chair.

The door was open now, and he had been right after all. Inspector Conway, followed by Sergeant Mayhew, was just coming into the hall. Alison Clive, in what appeared to be a state of extreme agitation, was backing away before them and saying ineffectually, 'You can't want to see Ellen. Not again. There can be no need.'

'I'm afraid—' began Conway, looking a little put out by this greeting. But he stopped when he saw Antony in the door of the drawing-room. 'I might have known!' he said.

'In here, Inspector,' Maitland invited. He hadn't much hope of being able to convince the detective, he might be letting himself in for a suit for slander, but at least once he had had his say his life, and Roger's, would be no longer in danger. And no-one would dare send threats to Jenny, for fear of seeming to confirm ...

'Miss Gray—?' Conway was saying.

'Mrs Clive will fetch her for us. You will, won't you, Mrs Clive? Miss Gray and Mr Langland. And come back to the drawing-room with them.' He was speaking as persuasively as he could, but he wasn't sure how much of what he said was penetrating her bewilderment. But as he looked at her a very faint hope began to stir in his mind. 'Come back to the drawing-room with them,' he said again.

'Very well.' She began to move towards the dining-room, and Conway took a step to follow her when he was halted by Antony's voice.

'Not that way, Inspector. In here. There's someone I want you to meet.' This time he spoke as with authority, but all the same he was astonished to see both the detectives move obediently in his direction.

While he had been absent Doctor Clive seemed to have pulled himself together. He came to meet them now, saying smoothly, 'I'm sorry you've been dragged into this, Inspector, but I think you can be of help to us. Mr Maitland appears to have gone mad.'

'That is not altogether unexpected. Not by me, at any rate,' said Conway, with what seemed to be a rather heavy attempt at humour. Mayhew gave his warning cough, which really sounded more than anything else like a grandfather clock nerving itself to strike, and said hollowly,

'If that's true, it's a pity. A great pity.' Antony turned and smiled at him and he maintained his sober look, but there was a glint of amusement in his eye.

Roger, still standing behind the stranger's chair, said into the small silence that followed, 'This chap has a gun.'

Conway was in the middle of the room now. He looked rather wildly from Antony to Doctor Clive, to the fair man sitting tranquilly in the chair he had occupied from the beginning. 'May I know your name, sir?' he said.

201

'Certainly. It is Matthew Darrow. Do I understand that you are an inspector of police?'

'I am. Detective Inspector Conway. This is Detective Sergeant Mayhew. Is there any truth in what Mr Farrell is saying?'

'Is that his name? No truth at all, Inspector. Would you like me to turn out my pockets?'

'Certainly not.' Conway, predictably, sounded outraged.

Darrow's smile grew warmer. 'Then may I ask your – your protection, Inspector? I was spending a quiet afternoon with my friend, William Clive, when these two gentlemen – previously unknown to me – came in and began making some rather odd accusations. They seem to think that *I* have been threatening *them.*'

Alison, and Ellen, and Stephen, came in then, and Sergeant Mayhew, who was standing by the door, shut it firmly behind them and then leaned on it. Darrow came to his feet, with what Antony considered an unnecessary display of good manners, and there was a period of confusion before the three newcomers were seated in a row on the long sofa that faced the fire. Darrow went back to his chair again, Doctor Clive resumed his seat, Antony sat down on the arm of the sofa close to Ellen Gray, and Conway remained standing in the midst of them with rather a school-masterish look on his face. 'Now then, what's all this about?' he asked.

'As I told you, Inspector—' Darrow began.

'Yes, I understand that,' said the inspector, rather shortly. 'It seems to me that before I can get on with what I came here to do some explanations are due from Mr Maitland.'

'With all the pleasure in the world,' said Antony lightly. Now it was coming, now he had to justify ... and he hadn't a hope in hell of convincing Conway, not one iota of proof ...

'You told me – no, to be exact, you implied – that the two men who stopped us in the square on Thursday evening were connected with the drug trade,' he said, addressing himself directly to the inspector. 'Well, our friend here, who calls himself Darrow ... I think he's what is known as a pusher.'

'I'm nothing of the kind.' There could be no doubt about it, Darrow was genuinely hurt by the description; though Conway would probably take it as moral indignation.

'I take it then,' Antony said, 'you're something much higher in the organisation.'

'That's a very serious charge, Mr Maitland,' said Conway frigidly.

'What's been happening is serious too. You won't have had time to hear about the flowers yet, that were delivered to Jenny, though I left my uncle telephoning when I came out.'

'Flowers?' echoed Conway. 'What's all this nonsense?'

'You may c-call it nonsense if you l-like.' But he mustn't lose his temper, that would be fatal. 'There was a note with them threatening a bomb "next time".'

'And you're accusing Mr Darrow—?'

'He was certainly the person who phoned me on Wednesday. Or have you forgotten about the phone call, Inspector? He may have been doing it on someone else's instructions; but I doubt it, having met him.'

'Besides,' said Roger, 'he admitted when we came in that he was here to discuss the best way of getting rid of us.'

'To discuss with Doctor Clive ... oh, this is too much!' said Conway in an overwrought way. He looked from Roger to Antony, and then back at Matthew Darrow again. 'These are the accusations you spoke of?'

'I'm afraid so,' said Darrow tranquilly. 'If only one

person were concerned ... but it seems rather an odd aberration that strikes two men at once.'

'You'd better begin at the beginning, Antony,' said Roger in a resigned voice. 'Then perhaps you can make the inspector understand.'

'I haven't time for all this nonsense,' said Conway snappishly. 'I came here—'

'I'm afraid you'll have to find time for it, Inspector,' Antony told him. 'I'm talking about conspiracy to murder. A complaint has been made and must be investigated.'

'There is also such a thing as the law of libel,' said Darrow, still infuriatingly composed. 'If you will leave matters here, Mr Maitland, I will make no complaint. But if you persist in this ridiculous charge—'

'I'm not afraid of a prosecution for slander, believe me. It would be one way,' said Antony, assuming a good humour he did not feel, 'of getting you into court.'

'Then I won't be answerable for the consequences,' said Darrow, with a sudden show of impatience. Maitland smiled at him.

'May I go on, Inspector?' he asked.

'If you insist, and if you aren't afraid of a slander suit,' said Conway, tight-lipped. 'But I should like to remind you, Mr Maitland, that obstructing the police is also a serious matter.'

'But I'm trying to help you.' Conway looked his scepticism. 'Really, Inspector!' he said, and smiled again.

Something about his smile made Roger uneasy, but he said only, 'From the beginning, Antony.' He was still standing behind Darrow's chair, but Darrow had not once glanced up at him.

'That would be to go back to 1945,' said Antony. Conway's scowl became blacker than ever. 'I think, on the whole, I'll start with what was really the beginning for me, and use the flashback system if I must. The beginning was when you came to see me, Mr Langland, last Sunday, and persuaded me that there was still a case for investigation. I wasn't very happy about it, not at all sure that Ellen was innocent, but I had – or thought I had – good grounds for thinking that perhaps Edward Gray hadn't been guilty after all. If that was so, and someone else killed Madeleine and Michael Foster, that same someone might have had a motive for the murder of John Wilcox. It was a starting point, the only one I could see, and if it were true the murderer must be someone whose acquaintance with the victims had lasted over a considerable span of years.'

Conway, who had been simmering gently, interrupted him there. 'May I remind you that I am interested only in the death of Mrs Frances Wilcox?'

'No, really, Inspector, you're not doing yourself justice. You're interested in the truth, aren't you?'

'Of course I am.'

'Then listen. It was Wednesday before I had time to do anything, and then I came here to see Doctor and Mrs Clive and Ellen, and later in the day Roger and I went to see Frances Wilcox. She told us one thing that might, or might not, be important ... that her husband had been a little thoughtful during the last days of his life.'

'That hardly seems significant, Mr Maitland.'

'Wait a bit.' He was into his stride now, completely absorbed by what he was doing. 'It was that same evening that Mr Darrow telephoned me, warning me to leave Ellen Gray's affairs alone. At the moment I didn't see the significance of that, which was foolish of me. I put it down to a crank, the kind of person who writes anonymous letters to anyone in the public eye, but what I didn't realise – though Jenny practically pointed it out to me – was that someone knew I'd re-opened the case,

205

and that had to mean Doctor Clive, Mrs Clive, Ellen herself, Stephen Langland, or Frances Wilcox. Or one of Mrs Wilcox's children, I suppose I should add, though for obvious reasons I wasn't considering the possibility of their complicity. But none of that occurred to me until after the two men accosted us in Kempenfeldt Square, and it was then that I first considered the possibility that Doctor Clive might be the villain of the piece.'

Ellen murmured something that could only have been a protest. William Clive sat up straighter in his chair and said indignantly, 'I can only agree with Matthew that you have gone mad, Mr Maitland. Apart from anything else, what possible motive could I have had?'

'I'd rather come to that in a moment, if you don't mind.' Antony turned to glance at Alison Clive, who was huddled at the other end of the sofa, but if she was attending to what he was saying it wasn't apparent. 'Up to that point, you see, I'd been thinking that either Frederick Tate or Martin Roydon must be the one, but I couldn't connect either of them with the warnings I was receiving because neither of them knew until I phoned them that I had re-opened the case. But I still wanted to see them, and Roger and I talked to Tate yesterday, and to Roydon today. What would you say we learned from them, Roger?'

Roger was startled by the question, coming as it did at a point when he was practically certain that Maitland was no longer aware of his presence. But Antony's train of thought when they had talked had been obvious enough, and if he thought the information would carry more weight coming from an independent source ... 'Roydon on the whole was the more informative,' he said, readily enough, 'but what Tate had to say backed him up, so far as it went. Madeleine Gray asked Roydon's advice over something that was worrying her.

Someone she knew and liked had – had committed a crime—'

'Had "done something dreadful",' Antony interposed.

'Yes, that was it. She had found out about it and wanted to know what to do. Roydon told her to talk to the person concerned. Then, a couple of days before John Wilcox was killed they all dined together—'

'All?' put in Conway stonily.

'John and Frances Wilcox, Frederick and Mathilda Tate, and Martin and Dorothy Roydon, to be precise,' Maitland told him. 'Go on, Roger.'

'The point about the dinner is that John Wilcox started a conversation about not being able to judge people by appearances, to which Tate contributed the expression "whited sepulchres", which apparently Wilcox took perfectly seriously. So there's a clear similarity of circumstances between the two first murders. And about Mrs Wilcox—'

'I'd better tell them that bit,' Antony interrupted him. 'You only heard it at second hand. But, of course, you know all about it already, Inspector. Frances Wilcox found her husband's diary the day before she died, and after her death it was missing.'

'It all seems a little far fetched,' said Conway.

'Not really. Madeleine Gray was worried about some knowledge she had acquired about someone she was fond of. She was killed two days after being advised to have it out with the person concerned.'

'You're forgetting Michael Foster.'

'No, I think his death could almost be called accidental. Whether or not Madeleine confided in him, he was killed because he was there.'

'It's a convenient theory, but—'

'I'm coming to John Wilcox next. He wasn't perhaps worried, but he had on his mind some person – man or woman – who wasn't all that he, or she, appeared to be. He may have given himself the advice that Martin Roydon gave to Madeleine, to confront the person concerned with his knowledge. If, later, Frances Wilcox learned what he knew from his diary—'

'That's far fetched, and you know it, Mr Maitland,' Conway said again.

'Why, then, is the diary missing?'

'It may well have recorded something that Wilcox knew, something that led to his own murder,' Conway conceded. 'But we're not concerned with that at the moment.'

'Oh, but I think we are. You're trying to say that Wilcox recorded something about Ellen, which led to his own death and later to his wife's murder. He certainly didn't sit there calmly making notes while Ellen waved a Mauser automatic at him, and if he had she as certainly didn't considerately hide the diary where it might later be found.'

'The motive for Wilcox's murder may not have been the one that was cited at the trial.'

'No, I don't think it was. But now we've established – don't you think? – a chain linking the three murders. And even if Ellen had been murderously inclined at eight years old, she could never have held a heavy gun steady enough to shoot two people dead.'

'It's a clever argument, certainly,' said Conway in a grudging tone. 'And all built out of nothing. Now, Mr Maitland, if you've finished—'

'Not quite. You're forgetting that Mr Farrell and I have laid an information about conspiracy to murder.'

'Which you have so far done nothing to substantiate,' snapped Conway, suddenly at the end of his patience.

Mayhew coughed, and said soothingly, 'Mr Maitland likes to take his time.'

'You're wrong for once,' Antony retorted. 'The sooner we can get this over with the better I'll be pleased.' He got up as he spoke, the instinct to move around the room proving too much for him, and drifted across to the window. 'We come now to the motive,' he said.

'And not a moment too soon,' said Conway pointedly.

'Very well, I'll be brief.' He came back again to stand near the end of the sofa where Ellen sat. 'I think that Mr Darrow is a dealer in drugs, and that Doctor William Clive has been acting for him for years as part of his distribution organisation.'

'I said you were mad,' said Doctor Clive forcefully. Darrow said nothing, but shook his head in a more-in-sorrow-than-in-anger way.

'I hope,' said Conway insincerely, 'that you can substantiate these claims, Mr Maitland.'

'Then you'll be doomed to disappointment. I can, however, tell you how I think it all started.' He moved forward as he spoke, until he stood at Conway's side, and turned to face the three people on the sofa. 'I think you, Mrs Clive, could tell us that: why you retired from medical practice, and why your husband, who loves you, found himself in need of an additional source of supply of morphine.'

Alison raised her head. He wasn't sure that she had been listening to him before, but now at least she was. 'I can tell you nothing,' she said, very quietly. Ellen jerked forward to lean across Stephen and take her aunt's hand.

'You don't have to say anything, Aunt Alison,' she said.

'Nothing at all, my dear,' Doctor Clive echoed her.

'Then I'll try to explain my train of thought.' Expect nothing and you wouldn't be disappointed. 'I looked up morphine, as I told you, Doctor Clive,' said Antony, 'and one of the things I learned about it was that an addict might present quite a normal appearance, provided that a constant supply was available and the drug level maintained. Nevertheless, it was noticeable from the few times I saw her, that Mrs Clive's spirits were subject to fluctuation. You could confirm that, Miss Gray, if you will.'

Ellen was leaning back in her own corner of the sofa now. She said, 'You're not doing this for me, Mr Maitland. I couldn't let you be so cruel.'

'I'm afraid it's not a matter of choice any longer. Even if I were inclined to listen to you – which I'm not, because I don't believe in all this self-sacrifice – even if I were inclined to listen to you,' he repeated, 'I wouldn't, because of the threat to my wife.'

'I don't understand that,' said Ellen bewilderedly.

'Mr Darrow felt threatened by the threat to Doctor Clive. It wasn't very imaginative of him to threaten me in his turn, because it served to confirm what I was only slowly coming to believe, that you were innocent, Miss Gray. But I wonder if Mrs Clive understands how I feel.' Alison slowly shook her head. He went forward then, and took her hand, which lay limply in his. 'Mrs Clive! You see how much your niece is prepared to do for you, but can you accept her sacrifice? It isn't just a family matter any more. The stone has been thrown, and the ripples are spreading. Four people have died—'

'Oh, no, no, no!' Her voice went higher with every word, and she snatched her hand away from his. 'I don't know what you're talking about, I don't know anything—'

'I'm talking about murder, Mrs Clive. If you didn't know at first—'

'I didn't. I didn't!'

'—you must lately have come to suspect what has been happening. And to ask Ellen to accept the consequences, as her father did unwittingly before her—'

'No, that isn't fair. It isn't fair, is it, Will?'

'This has gone far enough,' said Doctor Clive harshly. 'My wife's health is poor, Inspector—'

But Conway, for once in his life, seemed oddly in-decisive. 'You are under no obligation to answer Mr Maitland's questions, Mrs Clive,' he said. And then, 'A wife cannot be asked to give evidence against her hus-band, Mr Maitland,' he added, but undoubtedly he sounded regretful.

'Of course not, but if she does it of her own free will ... besides, this is a completely informal occasion, isn't it? But we're getting off the track, Inspector. The other thing I noticed was that Mrs Clive always wore long-sleeved dresses, which perhaps isn't surprising at this time of year, but still it tended to confirm what I was coming to believe.'

'I will not listen to another word of this!' said Doctor Clive, bouncing to his feet suddenly. Conway turned one of his cold looks upon him.

'I'm afraid you have no choice, doctor. Counter-accusations have been made and, as Mr Maitland has pointed out, they must be examined. Unless you would rather continue this discussion at the station—'

'That is an outrageous suggestion.'

'Not in the circumstances. What is the point you are trying to make, Mr Maitland?'

'I think – no, be quiet, Ellen, this has got to be said. I think Mrs Clive is a drug addict of many years' standing – most likely an addict of morphine, as I implied a few minutes ago. For a short time her husband himself would have been able to supply her needs ... there is nothing easier than for a doctor to cook his own books. But there must have come a time when the amount needed was beyond his means, and that, I think, is when he started to look for an alternative source of supply and fell in with Mr Darrow. How much further his involvement goes I cannot say, but I should imagine much further; men of Darrow's type do not lightly allow an obligation to go unexploited.'

'You draw a pretty picture of me, Mr Maitland,' Darrow was saying lightly, but Antony's attention was all for Mrs Clive, who had begun to sob quietly while he was speaking, and who was now fumbling with the buttons on her cuffs. 'I'll show you,' she said. 'It was all my fault, everything that happened. If it hadn't been for me—'

'Be quiet!' This time Doctor Clive's intervention was far from gentle. 'This is intolerable, Inspector.'

'I think we must let the lady have her say.' Conway's fascinated attention was also held by Mrs Clive. The cuff was unbuttoned now, and the sleeve rolled up, and there – plain for them all to see – were the marks of the hypodermic, so close that it was a wonder if room could be found for one more. Ellen caught her breath sharply, and leaned across Stephen to take her aunt's hand again. 'Don't!' she said. 'Don't!' Doctor Clive, his face ashen, had fallen back in his chair again. He might have been leaning back at his ease but it looked to Roger, the only one who had any attention to spare for him, more like a collapse. He could only see the top of Matthew Darrow's head, but he got the impression of wariness, of a snake that might be about to strike, and his own anxious vigilance increased. Antony, he knew, had no thought to spare for anything but his witness.

'But I must,' said Alison Clive. 'Because it's all my fault, you see, and if anyone should be punished—' She broke off there, and removed her hand, gently but quite firmly, from Ellen's clasp. 'If only I had never experimented but the craving was on me before Will knew, and what could he do then but help me? And even then it wouldn't have mattered, nobody would have suffered but myself, if only I hadn't told Madeleine. I must have been mad to do it, but sometimes the longing for sympathy was too much for me, but the information worried her, you see.'

'Aunt Alison!' Ellen was leaning forward now, trying

to face the other woman squarely. 'You mean you knew, all this time, that it wasn't my father—'

'Of course I knew! But what could I do, Ellen? You must see I couldn't do anything about it. It was Will's life at stake, and besides if they'd taken him away where could I have got the drug?'

'Oh, no!' Ellen looked from Antony to the Inspector and back again. 'Need we go on with this? I don't think I can bear it. I've loved them for so long, been grateful to them for so long—'

'I'm sorry,' said Antony. Conway said nothing, but his eyes never left Alison's face. Ellen turned, and hid her eyes against Stephen's shoulder.

'Go on, Mrs Clive,' Antony urged quietly. 'After a time you began to forget the result of that first indiscretion, didn't you?'

'I suppose that was it. Otherwise I should never have told John, should I? And he wasn't even sympathetic! He said I must see how foolish I was being. He said he'd talk to Will.'

'Did you tell John Wilcox where the morphine came from?'

'How could I? I didn't know, only that Will gave it to me, and it was none of my business where he got it from, was it?'

'But you did tell him—'

'She told him enough.' That was Doctor Clive. His voice had the harsh note they had heard before, but for all that it was steady. 'If he'd gone to the police there'd have been evidence.'

'Doctor Clive, I must warn you—' William Clive waited in silence while the familiar words were repeated, but then said almost impatiently,

'It doesn't matter. There's no hiding anything now, is there?'

'You killed John Wilcox?' Antony asked.

'John, and Frances. She was worried by something he'd written in his diary, enough to start an investigation if it had got into wrong hands. And, as I said, there'd have been evidence. Darrow always wanted his pound of flesh, damn him. I didn't have to pay for the morphine, but I paid in other ways.'

'How?'

'Have you ever thought how conveniently placed a doctor's surgery is for distributing drugs?'

Matthew Darrow spoke into the silence that followed that last remark. 'I'm sorry for what I've heard, of course. I consider Will Clive a friend of mine. But that he should follow this man Maitland's lead in trying to apportion some part of the blame to me is something beyond a joke.'

'Nevertheless, Mr Darrow—'

Conway broke off there when he realised that Roger was also speaking. 'It might be as well to have some confirmation of what we told you about the threats that were made, Inspector,' said Roger, and thrust his hand down so quickly into the right-hand pocket of Darrow's jacket that the fair man had no chance to resist. 'There!' said Roger in a pleased way, holding out the pistol. 'Evidence, Inspector. I think you should take charge of it.'

'Thank you,' said Conway in a dazed way. 'Have you—?' But for the second time he was destined to be interrupted.

'And while we're about it,' Roger said, holding Darrow down forcibly now with his left hand, 'there's something in his breast pocket.' Again his right hand moved swiftly, and emerged clutching a green oilskin pouch. 'Not pipe tobacco, I think,' he said triumphantly.

'Mr Farrell—' Conway protested faintly.

'Take it, see what you think,' Roger urged him.

'But—' All the same he took the package, and stood looking at it rather helplessly.

214

'It's all right.' Maitland was amused to see his friend momentarily in charge of the situation. 'You told me something about the Dangerous Drugs Act once, Antony. Something about arrest without a warrant.'

'Quite right, but the Inspector knows it already. If a person has committed an offence under the Act, or is reasonably suspected of having done so—'

Conway seemed to come to life. Darrow was still under Roger's hands now. The Inspector opened the pouch. 'White powder,' he said, and tasted a little on the tip of his finger. 'I'm not an expert,' he went on, 'but I think your grounds for reasonable suspicion exist, Mr Maitland.'

Mayhew stirred, and turned a little so that he could rest his hand on the door knob. 'Shall I phone the local station, Inspector?' he asked.

It was at that moment, to a scene of some confusion, that Geoffrey Horton arrived, all ready to represent his client, Miss Ellen Gray.

SUNDAY, 7th February

'If I understand you rightly, Antony,' said Sir Nicholas, looking over his audience for any signs of inattention, 'you laid yourself open to a suit for slander yesterday afternoon, if events hadn't turned out as they did, while Roger was lucky to get away without being charged with common assault.' He was having tea with the Maitlands, as was his almost invariable practice on a Sunday, and Roger and Meg were there too.

'Tell me how else we could have dealt with the situation,' said Antony amiably. He was both feeling and looking relaxed, as Jenny hadn't seen him for days, and all things considered Uncle Nick's comments could have been a great deal worse.

'Probably in no other way,' Sir Nicholas conceded. 'But the situation, may I remind you, was of your own making.'

'Something had to be done.'

'But that isn't important now, darlings,' said Meg, only too obviously rehearsing a role as peacemaker. 'You've told us what happened up to the time that odious Inspector Conway took over, but what has happened since?'

'Quite a lot.'

'Inspector Conway came to see us this morning,' Jenny put in. 'He was almost as severe as Uncle Nick is being about the awkwardness of the position into which he had been forced, but he was quite informative too.'

'I wish I'd been here,' said Roger.

'For my part, you'd have been welcome to the experience,' Antony assured him. 'I've known people I was fonder of than I am of the inspector.'

'The thing is,' said Meg, 'what did he say? I'm sure you're dying to hear, Uncle Nick,' she added cajolingly. Sir Nicholas smiled a grim smile, but said nothing.

'Jenny was here, she can tell you,' said Antony unhelpfully. At which Roger and Meg groaned in unison (Jenny was not noted for the clarity of her explanations) and even Sir Nicholas was moved to protest.

'If we must hear – and I can see we shall get no peace from Meg until we do – let it by all means be from you, Antony. Jenny should not be asked to put herself out on your behalf.' Antony sighed, but Jenny smiled to herself and folded her hands in her lap.

'Well,' said Antony, 'to quote you, Meg, the thing is that Doctor Clive has talked. And that being so, they should have no difficulty in obtaining sufficient evidence to sustain the charge against Matthew Darrow; though – and this is a reversal of what usually happens – they may not be able to lay hands on the people below him in the organistaion.'

'Assuming they exist,' Sir Nicholas put in.

'They exist all right, at least according to Conway. He's been talking to the narcotics people, of course.'

'At least,' said Meg, looking on the bright side, 'they probably won't be able to carry on without him.'

'Possibly not, but that isn't our worry. As I said, Doctor Clive talked.'

'Overcome by his feelings of guilt,' said Meg, registering remorse.

'I don't know about that. He seems to me to have been pretty cold-blooded about what he has done in the past. *I* think he knew the game was up once his wife began to go to pieces, and so made a virtue of necessity.'

'If we must hear this story,' said Sir Nicholas coldly, 'and perhaps if Meg will refrain from interrupting we may get along more quickly, let us at least refrain from the use of clichés.'

'I'll give him this,' said Antony, ignoring the interruption, 'I think he was genuinely in love with his wife, and it must have been agony for him all these years watching her slow deterioration.'

'There are places—' Meg began, but she caught Sir Nicholas's eye upon her, grinned impenitently, and relapsed into silence again.

'So there are, but she never felt she could face it – it isn't pleasant, you know – and he never felt he could force her into taking a cure. At first he dealt with the situation himself, and I'm afraid that a good many patients who should have been getting morphine were getting injections of plain water, and just when he was getting desperate as to how to falsify his records to provide the larger doses Mrs Clive was needing Darrow got in touch with him. Doctor Clive says he doesn't know how the fact that he was in the market leaked out, and Darrow isn't talking so I can't enlighten you on that point, but the deal was that the doctor should help in distributing the drug to a number of Darrow's "clients", and in return should be provided with whatever he needed for his wife's use. He says Mrs Clive never knew about the arrangement, thought he was supplying her himself as before, and that's probably true, at least at first. But she couldn't keep her mouth shut, one day she confided her addiction to Madeleine Gray, and Madeleine, not knowing anything about the larger issues, felt it her duty to talk to her cousin, to try and persuade him to send his wife for treatment. William Clive must have regarded even that limited knowledge as dangerous, because once questions were asked there was so much more to be found out. So when he had completed his plans he killed her, and Michael Foster too, just because he happened to be there. He never knew anything until later of Edward's return, having used the side entrance to the block of flats where the Grays lived. He talks about the mental anguish of knowing Edward was accused, but I think he just felt he'd got out of everything rather well. Certainly he was even more ready to kill when next the same thing happened. But in the meantime he was genuinely kind to Ellen. You know, I liked him, until I began to realise ... he was clever at masking his feelings. And I still don't know: did he, or didn't he, want Ellen convicted?'

'Mrs Clive kept silent for quite a number of years. Do you suppose she guessed what had happened?' asked Meg.

'She more or less admitted it, but her dependance on her husband was enough to ensure her silence.'

'But not to ensure her silence about her own failing,' said Roger, with an apologetic glance at Sir Nicholas. 'I take it that's how John Wilcox found out.'

'Apparently, and he, I should imagine, would be more alive to the possibilities than Madeleine was. Still, even a hint of knowledge of Alison's addiction would have been enough to sound the alarm and Clive reacted accordingly. Wilcox, you see, apparently gave himself the same advice as Roydon had given Madeleine all those years ago ... talk to your friend first, give him a chance to amend matters. And so the stage was set for another tragedy.'

'There's one thing that worried me when you were talking to the inspector, and that worries me still,' Roger admitted. 'Wasn't it rather a coincidence that a gun of the same type should be missing at the hand gun club?'

'I'm glad you didn't mention it at the time, because I couldn't have given you the answer, but I can now. Ellen, as you remember, was at the club on the Monday evening and heard about the windfall the secretary had had, and that he had put the newly-acquired pistol in his desk until he could see to the licensing. Somehow or other the subject came up at breakfast the next morning. Ellen says she thought it would be interesting to try a completely different type of gun from anything she had tried before, and so she mentioned it. The doctor therefore went round to the club the same evening asking for membership under an assumed name. The secretary left him in his office filling in a form, which was just what Clive had hoped would happen—'

'But he couldn't count on that,' Meg objected.

'No, but if he wasn't left alone he would have been no worse off, so it was worth trying. As it was he went away with the gun in his pocket, and took his half-complete form with him at the same time. The secretary thought it was a bit odd, but soon forgot all about it – that bit's supposition, but he never noticed the gun was gone until later, of course.'

'Was Doctor Clive trying to involve Ellen?' asked Jenny in a troubled voice.

'I don't think so, love, though, as I said, I can't be sure. I don't think it ever entered his head that she might be suspected, but when he knew she was going to see Wilcox that night he thought he must get there ahead of her. That's another thing, when I was beginning to suspect him; it was a bit of a coincidence if someone had shot Wilcox just before Ellen had got there, but what if it wasn't a coincidence at all? If Uncle Nick will forgive me, *conscience doth make cowards of us all*, and the doctor thought if they got talking together Wilcox might begin to put two and two together about Madeleine's death. So Clive rushed out of the house on Ellen's heels, saying there was a patient he'd promised to see. And the way things worked out ... well, he seemed to think we couldn't really blame him for letting his niece take the consequences.'

'I don't think I like your Doctor Clive very much,' said Meg thoughtfully, and Jenny added with indignation in her voice,

'It just makes him worse, being such a hypocrite. I mean, Antony, he'd been good to Ellen, taking her in when her father was sent to prison. And she was grateful and didn't want to give him away.'

'I don't think she went so far as to suspect him of murdering John Wilcox. She'd got his integrity so firmly fixed in her head,' Antony told her. Jenny didn't really like thinking anybody particularly villainous, and he spoke in a reassuring tone. 'Ellen didn't think the police would suspect him, but she thought I might.'

'Your unfortunate reputation,' sighed Sir Nicholas.

'Yes, well, she did tell me the truth at last; and what is more important, repeated it to Conway when he asked her.'

He seemed to have finished there, until Roger prompted him. 'There's another awkward point, you know, Antony. Mrs Wilcox was poisoned with morphine.'

'You mean, how did he persuade her to take it?'

'That's it.'

'Well, he went there in response to her urgent request, he told Conway this himself, and found her puzzling over something her husband had written in his diary. He says he didn't find it difficult to convince her that there was nothing in the entry that concerned him. Wilcox had written something like, "heard a strange tale today from Alison. Can't believe it in its entirety, but must ask Will about it". So the doctor just talked about delusions, said his wife had suffered from them for years and they were getting worse. Then Frances began telling him about our visit, Roger, so he said he could see she was upset and wouldn't she take a tranquilliser, and when she agreed he gave her the morphine to take.'

'I wonder he bothered, if she believed him.'

'Remember, he'd killed twice already, and the generally accepted view seems to be that it gets easier each time. She might have thought things over after he had gone and come to a different conclusion ... that's what he says, anyway. So he gave her the morphine in tablet form, and left it to take effect after he had gone. He had to resort to poison because he had no weapon to hand this time.'

'Couldn't Darrow—?'

'But he was in a hurry to deal with the matter ... couldn't wait.'

'So Mrs Wilcox died alone,' said Jenny in a sombre voice; and Meg, who was almost as protective as Antony on occasion, took her up quickly.

'I don't suppose it was any worse than falling asleep.'

'But it was ... I don't think I shall ever feel quite the same about doctors again,' said Jenny stubbornly.

'If you must dwell on the case, love, look on the bright side,' Antony suggested.

'Is there one?'

'Oh, come now!'

'What about Mrs Clive?' Jenny retorted.

'Yes, what about her, darling?' Meg echoed, not without a certain malicious pleasure in feeling she was catching him out.

'You would bring that up, and I admit I don't suppose she's enjoying life much at the moment. She's under arrest, but in hospital, of course. They can't just leave her without the drug altogether, or she'd go mad.'

'But now she says she didn't know anything,' said Meg.

'Yes, but she admitted enough during our session yesterday to substantiate a charge as accessory. However, I don't think it's absolutely certain that they'll press the matter in view of her state of health, even if it is self-induced.'

'I hope not,' said Jenny. Sir Nicholas, who had been watching her, said into the brief silence that followed,

'Where's this bright side you promised us, Antony?'

'Well . . . Ellen.'

'She seemed pretty upset to me,' Roger reminded him.

'So she was. But at least she's in the clear now. And when I talked to her this morning she sounded much better. Stephen wants to get married immediately, so she's staying with the Wilcox children until he can make the arrangements.'

'In fact,' said Meg, 'everything is for the best—' But this was too much for Sir Nicholas.

'The most that can be said,' he remarked repressively, 'is that some good – a small amount of good – has come out of evil.'

Antony muttered, 'Who's talking in clichés now?' but Meg's protest overbore him.

'Uncle Nick, darling,' she said, 'you can't disapprove of criminals getting their deserts.'

'Nor do I. I was referring,' said Sir Nicholas, looking round again to make sure his audience was with him, 'to the extraordinary manner in which the matter was dealt with. When I think—'

'Have some more tea, Uncle Nick,' said Jenny in a hurry, and Sir Nicholas, with one of his sudden reversals of mood, said benignly,

'By all means, my dear,' and held out his cup to be filled.